JONAS

Darkness #7

K.F. BREENE

Copyright © 2014 by K.F. Breene

All rights reserved. The people, places and situations contained in this ebook are figments of the author's imagination and in no way reflect real or true events.

❦ Created with Vellum

SYNOPSIS

Jonas isn't the kind of guy to submit to the expectations of others, even when his life is on the line. So when he wakes up in the cell of a dungeon with torture devices hanging on the wall, he can only think one thing: this should be fun. What he didn't expect, however, is the beautiful but broken female pitting herself against his resolve. For once, the pain of his past is shallow in comparison to another, and he wants nothing more than to extinguish her pain.

When Sasha realizes one of her own has been taken, the gloves come off. Using her ever-expanding resources of both human and non-human magic workers, she sets out to battle the most advanced, most experienced magic worker in the world. Regardless of being completely outmatched, Sasha and Stefan rush to Jonas' aid.

CHAPTER ONE

Jonas blinked his eyes open and minutely shook his head. Throbs of pain pulsed behind his forehead. He felt rough stone under his bruised knees. His wrists were secured behind his back with unyielding metal. Pulling his arms apart, then twisting, had the shackles biting into his skin. A trickle of liquid dribbled into his palm. Blood.

He remembered feeling eyes on him at the *Mata* compound. The feeling of being watched had tickled between his shoulder blades. He'd looked around, then behind him, to see if one of the mangy shifters was staring at him. Except for a distant wolf at the far end of the perimeter, though, no one had been around.

He'd recalled the tricks of magic that could make a person invisible two seconds before a rough voice said, "Don't kill him—we can use him." Something dull had crashed down on his head before all went dark. Only someone with advanced use of magic could create and use an invisibility spell. Plus, that accent had been English. Jonas didn't know much about that pansy country, but he knew the irritating speech when he heard it.

It seemed they had out-of-town visitors. Probably here to cash in on all the problems with the Council. He couldn't blame them—he'd heard that Cato had tried a similar takeover method when the English and French were battling each other. He couldn't blame them, but he could sure kill them for thinking his country was defenseless.

As soon as he got free, that was.

Jonas looked around. He knelt in the middle of a square room made of old stone. Mold grew in cracks on the walls and across the floor. A damp, musty smell lingered in the air. There was one window, way up high at the top of the far wall, indicating most of this room was underground. An old basement probably, and not even remotely close to the health code standards.

Jonas heaved a laugh. He wiggled his arms again, hearing the clink of chain. He tried to move his feet, half-numb from being in this position for however long, and heard the same jingle. He was probably secured to the floor. His torso leaned against a thin strip of metal—a bar that made up a side of a rectangle. The two ends were braced into the floor to hold him up. Awfully nice of them, giving him something to lean on. He wondered why he wasn't secured to that, though.

There was a stone seat next to the wall in front of him, and one on the side. The other wall was bare. He glanced behind him. In the back, right corner was a stand gleaming with well-polished tools. Flays, whips, paddles, spikes—this was the makings for a great time. Jonas had a similar array in his quarters at the Mansion.

As a smile graced his lips for the shock the torturer would get when his version of torture wasn't going according to plan, the door behind him opened with a metallic wheeze. Two clicks announced someone in high heels before the door latched, the metallic sound echoing through the chamber.

Soft leather slid against wood, which clinked off of metal, in that back corner.

The torturer had arrived. And it was either a cross-dressing male, or a female.

He would have fun with either.

The clicks sounded again, coming around his body and stopping directly in front of him. A female, small for one of their kind, stood in front of him with a blank expression that didn't adequately hide the tightness around her eyes. She wore a red leather corset, black fishnet stockings, and shiny black heels. A pony tail held her glossy brown hair high on her head. Expertly manicured fingernails clutched her weapon of choice, a whip. Her features were straight and dainty, and her lips were a plump, bright red. She would be really hot if she wasn't trying too hard—if the female was any more rigid, she'd have to pull the stick out of her ass to sit down.

She obviously felt inadequate in what she wore, but that hold on the whip gave Jonas shivers. Very pleasant shivers. She balanced it delicately in a sure, comfortable grip. Confidence radiated in the light touch she had with that weapon. The expertly-worked leather was well-maintained—probably oiled and looked after on a regular basis. It would slash and cut in all the right ways.

Jonas let his gaze drift back up to her face. Her eyes were a clear blue and sparkling with intelligence. Currently, she was surveying his body and tracing his scars with her gaze. Trying to find his weaknesses. Trying to figure out how hard he really was—how easily he would break.

He'd been the subject of this type of scrutiny his whole life. Only, usually the one in control wore a sneer. In contrast, the gleam in her eyes bent more toward analysis.

Jonas felt a thrill of anticipation. So few females knew how to properly dominate. So few people in general, actually, females or males. He'd really only found one who could take him away from the encroaching wildness in his emotions and reset him. Make him someone that could exist with others without randomly sticking knives in people or throwing them through walls. But she had to struggle to dominate him on a regular basis. She wasn't as strong as she pretended to be, and she didn't understand the hardware as well as she needed to.

Most people probably didn't look forward to a torture session like he was. But by the look of it, this female could handle that whip. And he wanted to see what she was made of. He had a feeling she was a natural, and his experienced eye told him she'd had a lot of practice. Two good things.

As the heat started to burn in him, he recognized a shadow slowly creep into her gaze. The sparkle in her eyes started to ebb. Her body stiffened even more.

His arousal made her uncomfortable. Yet... she was wearing a corset. And liked to play with whips. What was this female playing at?

Jonas filed that information away as she started to speak in a low, sensual voice. "By now I imagine you know you've been taken. All we require out of you is information. Just a few easy answers and everyone is happy. You don't need to see me any more than is absolutely necessary."

She paused expectantly. Jonas simply stared. He was getting bored.

"So let's start with the easy ones, shall we?" She sauntered closer. As her shoes clicked on the stone she snaked the whip over her shoulder and then down across her body, eyeing the places on his torso her first strikes would land. That leather traveled over well-rounded breasts and delicious cleavage before sliding down her flat stomach and over shapely thighs. She was getting ready, not trying to entice him sexually. Her brutality was coming to the surface.

Jonas' heart started to hammer. That light of confident

ruthlessness sparkled in her eyes as she ran her finger lightly over the handle of her whip. Her pink tongue ran over that sensuous bottom lip before she smiled a little to herself. She was probably planning to punish him for his earlier arousal—probably going to teach him a lesson.

Oh gods, he really hoped she was planning to punish him. For a long time. Really hard.

He opened and closed his fists in anticipation.

"What's your name?" she asked in a sultry voice.

Jonas let his gaze burn into hers. Without flinching, tightness around her eyes completely gone, rigidity having melted in a graceful sensuousness that could not be taught, she met his gaze with a wild streak of raw violence. This female was stepping onto the battle field and her energy soaked into him like a power line. Jonas' dick was so hard he was having trouble thinking.

"I usually will not ask a question twice without something to fill the pauses. However, since this is your first time, I'll be lenient. Just this once." She stopped right in front of him. Her whip dangled down her thigh. "What is your name?"

Jonas watched her blue eyes flash. *Here it comes.*

She moved with the grace of a predator. Her hand came up quickly and *flicked*. The whip splashed out in a string of leather and licked his torso. A stinging pain he barely registered lanced his pec. She was taking it easy on him.

Damn.

"What is your name?" she asked again. He could hear the passion in her voice. The desire to inflict pain humming deeply in her words. But when the next lash fell, it was barely harder than the last.

His ardor started to drain away in his disappointment. She should've been able to tell what he could take by sizing him up—any torturer worthy of the title had that trait. And she probably did notice it—it seemed like she had by that analytical gaze—but she didn't act on it. She had the ability, but not the gumption.

What damned, depressing news.

Jonas let his gaze drift straight ahead toward the wall. Her sensual voice droned on as Jonas let his mind drift to Sasha and the Boss. He wondered how the little babies were. He wasn't a people person, but he'd always loved kids. They were so sweet and innocent when they were young. They looked at the world with big, bright eyes. Anything was possible. Jonas really wanted his own someday. He wanted a mate he could protect and support. A family to raise and a home away from the Mansion where he could spend his dawnings. He wanted peace, both of mind and body. Tranquility.

A whip stroke fell, the slice across his chest barely registering. He completely ignored any that came after—it wasn't hard to do.

He thought back to holding Sabrina when she was just a few hours old. He'd almost felt that tranquility he craved. That deeper purpose. Looking on her tiny, angelic face, he'd let go of his own demons. All he could think about was wanting to give everything he had to make sure Sasha's two infants went through life with the best it had to offer. They wouldn't be picked on and torn apart like he was. They'd have someone to stand up for them—to protect them, even if their parents took off. Jonas would make sure they were nothing but loved and supported, no matter what came.

The bite of the leather sank in a little deeper. Not just a housefly, now. A horse fly. Still irritating. He almost wanted to tell her to just move on to a knife—she wasn't fulfilling his expectations with the whip.

"Just your name. That's all I want."

He barely stopped himself from rolling his eyes as he let the caress of the leather lull his mind. Every torturer wanted to break their subject. That was the point. The beginning was an answer to a simple question. Just one answer. That wasn't so bad, the subject would think. The reprieve of pain would be a nice change. Then the next answer. And the next. When the pain got really bad, those answers were a lifeline until suddenly, the tortured was nothing more than a broken snitch. He was a dog, trained to obey.

That just didn't fly with Jonas. Plus, he'd been through all this before. It hadn't mattered that the boys who caught him were just pretending—their knives were real. The blood and pain was real. And he'd squealed. He'd squealed like a little pig. He'd told on his good friend for taking Julia's sword. He'd told on himself for a million things he shouldn't have done. He'd made stuff up. He'd pissed himself. He'd cried and begged. He'd promised them he'd do anything, *anything* if they'd let him go.

He'd been twelve. A child. The boys had been graduating school—much older than him. He'd been their first victim and he'd had to endure five different sessions before they'd gotten bored with him. They'd gotten caught when the next boy told on them. The other boy hadn't been afraid to speak up and became an instant martyr. Instead of shunning him, the adults all thought he was brave for enduring the torture.

No one ever knew Jonas had endured worse. He'd been too embarrassed to say anything.

"That's all for today. Tomorrow maybe you'll come to your senses."

It took Jonas a moment to realize the light pain had stopped. He looked around in confusion, only catching the female wiping off her whip at the far wall and hanging it up carefully. He glanced down at his chest. He had two gashes, and a great many welts.

The pain of his memories was what lingered, however. Physical pain would diminish in time. His past wouldn't. And hadn't.

CHAPTER TWO

"Where the hell is Jonas?" I roared. Panic threatened to overcome me. I stared at the collected group of Watch members all gathered around the large oval table in the strategy room. Stefan and Jameson stood at the head of the room, quietly watching me. Charles stood in the back corner, his eyes grim, his face a mask of rage. Paulie stood at my back, hands at his sides, just watching. He could look terrifying just doing that.

"My family member has been taken. I do not care that he is not blood—he is *mine*. I want him back. What are we doing to find him?" I demanded.

Yes, Stefan was supposed to lead these types of meetings. This was his territory. But when the guy we caught said we shouldn't be too hard on him, because then his guys would kill Jonas, I'd gone a little berserk.

"We know that they are English. We know that they think shifters are lowly mongrels, and we know they think humans are even worse than that—that captive really does hate humans." I paced the front of the room. I could get away with not being composed—I was more dangerous in this state of mind and everyone knew it. They also appreciated it, being a warrior race. "This means they will treat humans like you guys used to treat humans. They will use their pheromones, take them as blood donors and playthings, then kill them or just dump them off somewhere. So we are looking for an area steeped in ghost stories. An area where people, especially street people—" I gave a poignant glance back at Paulie, "will warn others to stay away from. A place that people get picked up, and then turn up a few days later talking about being used for sex and loving it. Something like that. People do not like when days go missing—they'll tell their friends. People also do not like when someone talks about paranormal activity—those who hear the stories will think the storytellers are nut jobs. All of this will be circling around the town. All we have to do is listen."

"The problem is, we don't know which town," Stefan said in a harsh voice. He did not like that one of his people was in enemy hands. Killing boiled in his dark eyes. "I put in requests immediately after he was taken to speak to the territories around this one. They've ignored me so far, however, and if I just show up, they'll take it as an act of war."

"Why?" I asked with my hands on my hips.

"Because they know I am outgrowing my post here. I've gotten more than a few challenges in my day to break off sections of my already larger-than-most territory. The territory leaders don't trust me. They know I can gain an even larger territory if I truly desired. They'll assume I want to carve out a bigger territory, and they will act defensively."

"God your people are paranoid. And asinine. And no, I don't need you comparing yourselves to humans—we are, too. I get it." I turned to Paulie. "That leaves your network of criminals."

"They're already on it. I'm working with Tim's people—he's got a pretty good network himself," Paulie answered in his rough gravel. He was new to this life, and the Mansion, and his magic, but he was already an active member of the Watch and extremely useful. His network of street people, all in their own gangs and only moonlighting for him because of the money and because he had no affiliation with anyone, were turning out to be damned useful.

"I'll get Birdie and her witches to start spreading out," I said. "They need to make friends with the New Age people in other cities, anyway."

"It amazes me how useful humans are becoming," Jameson reflected as he surveyed Paulie and me hashing out a rough plan. "It opens up a whole network of information. Just think if they could all use their magic, too."

"That's what Cato is planning," I muttered. Then snapped my fingers. "Why haven't I called him?"

"Dominicous is meeting with him in person," Charles reminded. Charles had lost his sense of humor when we'd realized Jonas had been taken. They didn't get along all that well, but it was clear that Charles thought of him as a brother. His eyes were grim and his body rigid. Flashes of light gold flared in his tattoos. He was ready to battle.

We all were. Jonas may be widely feared, but he was also widely respected. And he was ours. End of story.

"Oh yeah." I rubbed my temples. "He and Toa took that English guy and the shifter to Cato. Okay, then let's get people out there." I touched everyone with a glare. "Secure our territory, and get the eyes and ears out. He can withstand a lot of pain, as we know, but this is still going to suck for him. We want to get him out of harm's way as fast as possible."

I got a chorus of, "Yes, Mage," before I turned my eyes to the guy that would actually organize things. Stefan caught the glance and imperceptibly nodded. He and Jameson advanced to the map as worry started to fog over me again.

I didn't have a lot of family, but I'd be damned if the few people I'd come to know and love would be hurt in any way. I couldn't stand the idea of it. Especially after becoming a mother, I felt the cords of those I held dear as solid things attaching us together. Each second Jonas was missing caused me pangs of fear and pain. I was ready to storm the walls of hell to get him back.

I just needed to find the location of those walls.

"Well, how are we today?"

Jonas came out of his bored stupor as the door clunked shut. He lifted his head as something rattled behind him. He didn't bother to turn. He simply waited for the click-click of high heels to faux-saunter in front of him.

This was the fourth time in two days he'd seen this female. She always wore a leather corset, and she always tried to lather him with sex seconds after she walked in. She hated it, though; Jonas could tell. She hated every bit of that stupid act. It was in the way her eyebrows furrowed when he showed arousal. In the relief when he showed disinterest. In the rigidity of her body when he looked down at his hard-on, then pointedly looked back at her. And, most importantly, in the aggression of her whipping after the hard-on incident—which was actually quite fun.

She wasn't the only torturer in this room. She wasn't the only one trying to glean information. But she was the only one who kept losing control of her emotions. It didn't happen often, or for long periods of time, but he was chafing her emotions whereas she was just making him bleed. She didn't have the upper hand, and therefore, she didn't have the power.

He could tell it was starting to frustrate her. Obviously

most men didn't react the way he did. And her bosses could not have been pleased.

"Not even going to have a pleasant conversation?" she asked as she stopped in front of him. Stress lines gathered around the corners of her eyes. Suppressed emotion tugged down the edges of her lips.

Oh no, the bosses couldn't have been pleased. He hadn't uttered one word, or even one grunt, since he woke up in this place. If they wanted vital information, they picked up the wrong male.

The beautiful female waved a leather flaying device. The ends, coated in metal spikes, tinkled as they rubbed against each other. She was getting serious, thank the gods. It had taken long enough.

"Do you know what this is?" she asked in that naturally soft, sultry voice. The deeper feminine tones gave him a shiver. "This is my coercer. I can do more damage with a whip, but it'll peel away all your skin. We'll save that for when I don't need you anymore. Can't have you unconscious so early in the game, can we?"

She stepped forward with a hard swing. The splash of leather tipped with metal raked across his sensitive chest. The pain clawed at him.

Oh yeah, he'd feel this one.

He turned his gaze to the far wall, fixed it, and got ready to settle into the pain.

"Just tell me your name. That's all I want—the name of a handsome man. What is your name?"

After a silent pause, the rake of pain once again descended. He felt blood well up and overflow from a handful of wounds.

"What is your name?" she purred.

The rake of pain turned from claws into knives. They slashed into his chest and zinged through his body. Lava erupted from his skin and spread across his chest. Blood oozed from stinging gashes. A red haze clouded his vision.

Now we're getting somewhere.

He let his muscles relax totally. Let his awareness seep into the pain.

"What is your name?" she purred again.

He held onto that erotic voice as the next wave of agony washed through him. He sank down into it. Let it consume him.

Another hum of that beautiful voice. Another scrape of cruelty.

The tide pulled him under. He soaked it up and let it blend with his memories. Each slap of steel took the bite away from his memories. Transferred the pain from his past to his physical body. Let him feel the anguish externally so it would then fade away; the suffering of his memories would fade with it. At least for a while.

Steel slashed into his skin. Images of his mother leaving him wafted up. Of hearing her call him a worthless runt and walking out the door. She hadn't even secured a mate to take care of him. Or given him to anyone. She'd just walked out that door and never come back.

"What is your name?" the voice cooed. As soft and sweet as a dove.

The scour of torture was as biting and deep as an electric shock.

A male took him in, even though Jonas was small and scrawny for his age. Even though his mother had been low in power. Even though no one thought he'd amount to much. That male took him in and called him son. Gave Jonas a father. Gave him another family.

The bite of metal didn't erase the echoing pain from hearing his father had fallen because of that demon. The blood oozing down his chest didn't detract from the internal suffering of *knowing* he could've helped. He could've sacrificed himself for his father, if nothing else. He could've shown his father he was worth something. That he could grow up to be someone his father would be proud of. He could've mattered to someone.

He'd lost another family member. He should've been able to help.

Another burst of pain welled up, but this time inside of him. Jonas growled with it, fighting. The sear on his skin gave him something to latch onto. Gave him a place to direct the anguish. He attached his inner turmoil to the tears across his skin. To the pain infusing his body. To the misery that would heal with time.

"What is your name?"

That exotic voice hypnotized him. It sounded American, but there was a lilt to it. Almost as if she had a slight accent she didn't always use.

"What is your name? Tell me your name and this will all stop. Just your name. That won't betray anyone."

The silence rang in his ears. Crying welled up from deep in his memories. His sobs from his childhood. The kids taunting him. Picking on the weakest. The lowest in magic. The scrawny nobody whose own mother didn't want him.

You're no better than a human!

Look at the freak!

His arms are the size of a human's!

Was your real father a human? Is that why you can't do magic?

What are they going to do with you? You can't even work a sword.

Jonas welcomed the next flash of pain. And the next. He gritted his teeth, squinted his eyes shut, and owned it. Owned the pain. Owned his past.

He had gotten a growth spurt. He'd packed on forty pounds of muscle in one year. When he was in his last year at school, he got a heaping of strength, power and magic. All at once. And because he'd never given up, and had worked hard every day in his father's memory, to show he was worthy of being adopted by such a great male, he was suddenly the best in the class. And because of his classmates' constant taunts, he was also the meanest.

The meanest, most vicious fighter in that whole damn school.

Until he'd met Stefan. And Jameson. They were a year ahead, had recently graduated, and just as mean. Just as tough. And just as wild. Jonas didn't know what battles they'd had, but within the three of them, each found a kindred spirit. And they'd fought their way to the top. They'd shut everyone up and then kept them silenced.

Jonas ate up the pain in his aching body. He conquered it. And then internalized it once more. He wasn't a weak little bitch, anymore. He didn't take shit. He wasn't afraid of pain.

Jonas opened his blazing eyes and found the female staring down at him with wide eyes and an open mouth. He knew what she saw. A male kneeling on the floor with his hands tied behind his back looking as patient as if he were waiting at a bus stop. Even though blood ran down his chest, he showed no visible signs of pain. In fact, he bet he looked as tranquil as Sasha's beautiful babies after they'd been fed.

Her gaze slipped down to his crotch.

Oh yeah, and he was mightily turned on. This wasn't the feigned arousal like he'd worked up before to test her. This was a rock-hard erection that needed a beautiful female to sit in his lap. To take this triumph over his past and turn it into shared pleasure.

He locked eyes with her and begged her to touch him. To share this moment with him. To show him an act of love to further erase the pain.

Her eyebrows dipped low in confusion. She didn't look

away, but uncertainty had snuck into her gaze. Wariness mixed with curiosity. That shadow was back in her blue eyes. "That'll be all for today. I'll send someone in to clean you up."

Jonas followed her with his gaze as she hurried to the back wall and hastily hung up her tool. She ripped the door open and was out a moment later.

The torturee had unsettled the torturer. It probably wasn't her best day.

Jonas rolled his shoulders. He felt good. Really good. When she got going, she was dynamite with her tools. When she really let loose, so did he. He liked it.

He'd finally found what he'd always been looking for—just his luck she was the enemy.

CHAPTER THREE

Emmy paused with a splayed hand against the heavy wooden door. Her body trembled from top to bottom. That wasn't normal. What she'd just witnessed wasn't something that graced her inner chambers. Men with that much raw courage and confidence usually died in battle. They were rarely taken. And when they were, they just dealt with it in silence. They buckled down, clenched their teeth, and waited to die.

This man didn't wait to die. He welcomed the pain. He welcomed torture, almost as if it was a cure for something even worse that held him prisoner.

What sort of people did he come from that the level and precision of pain she could inflict aroused him?

The sort within these walls. The sort I report to.

Emmy straightened up and lifted her chin. She adjusted the too-tight corset and tried to suck in a steadying breath. The clothing was terribly uncomfortable and the tights belonged with a Halloween costume. She could fathom nothing sexy about her outfit.

Yet it usually did the trick. Turned men on right before she rained down the blows. Rage, arousal, powerlessness, loss of control—it was usually a recipe for near-immediate submission among males. Their egos couldn't handle the whiplash and they usually broke down in a matter of days.

Emmy smoothed out her corset and walked straight ahead. She had to mix it up. She had to analyze her subject and find his weaknesses. He wasn't like most, fine. But he was still a living creature. And all living creatures had self-destruct buttons. She would not let her perfect record be overturned by this man. That was not acceptable.

She walked through the lower tunnels with a whirling mind. At the steps leading to the ground floor, she nodded to a guard and ignored the sneer she got back. She waited for the door to be completely opened before walking through, paying no attention to his roaming eyes.

She really did hate this outfit.

Walking through the busy ground floor, she kept her eyes straight ahead and her body to the side. Even still, she saw passers-by swerve minutely so their larger bodies could bump and jostle her. She scraped the wall on more than one occasion, but didn't slow. To show weakness meant to get treated as weak. And though she didn't have a whip on her at the moment, if anyone challenged, she'd get one, and then beat them back. Whips were longer than swords. And she was damn good with them.

She'd proven that in this place.

She climbed the next set of stairs, continued down the corridor and finally turned into the sanctuary of her own room. Her sigh of relief was cut short. Sitting in the corner at her desk was the fair-headed Nathanial. When he heard the door open he stood with utter grace and fluidity.

Her hand twitched, missing the solidity of the whip in her hand. With that thought, she glanced at the far wall and found it there, hanging where she'd left it.

"Be at ease. You shall not need to defend yourself." He

walked toward her in slow, even steps. A condescending smile tweaked his lips. "Yet."

"Yes, sir." She stared at the far wall as his body came within inches of hers. His breath fell across her face. Cold fingertips trailed across her cleavage.

Her body tightened up, but she did not flinch. She did not try to shake away the crawling sensation of those disgusting fingers. Instead, she kept looking straight ahead at that wall. Waiting for it to stop. Waiting for him to go away. Or waiting to make herself numb if he chose to progress his touch.

"You no longer recoil from me." He took his hand away and sauntered toward the whip. He caressed it. "You are learning."

"Yes, sir."

"Did you make any strides with our captive?" His tone was light. Mocking.

"I took to him with three times the pain. Most men would've passed out. He smiled. He is not like most men that come through here. I need to come up with a different strategy for breaking him."

Nathanial turned to regard her slowly. His short-cropped blond hair framed a stony but handsome face. His eyes, which could be mistaken for beautiful with their sunburst of color, burned with a cold viciousness she'd seldom seen in another. He was a ruthless killer with absolutely no regard for life and less regard for humans. He'd smile at his oldest friend and then stab a knife in his gut.

That had happened when Nathanial had learned his favorite spy was taken by a mere human. And this right after his pet dog—a shifter—had been killed.

"Have you received *any* information?" Nathanial asked in a soft voice.

The small hairs along Emmy's arms rose. "Not yet. Like I said, he is—"

He moved with incredible speed. Before she could flinch away, his fist smashed across her cheek. Her head whipped to the side and her body followed, crumpling to the ground. She knew better than to get up.

"I did not ask for excuses," he said in the same soft voice. "I need results. We cannot get close to their encampment. Their dogs smell us and their mage has been able to unravel all of our most intricate spells of illusion—"

"The human?" Emmy asked with a sneer despite herself.

His foot cracked into her ribs with unreal force. Pain blistered along her side. Her breath came out in fast pants as she struggled with the tide of pain.

"Get results, or I will let you become a blood source again."

"No," she wheezed. "I'm only *half* human. The rules are that you cannot enslave your own kind!"

"Your human side negates any ties to us. Your mother was a fool for allowing you to be raised among our kind. It has put silly ideas in your head." He stepped closer and leaned over her. "Get answers. Or I will start taking you again before I pass you around."

Emmy couldn't help the shuddering breath as the door closed a moment later. She thought of running. She was in America, now. She had an American passport for the human world—her father had made sure of it. She could escape and blend in here. Start a life as a human.

Her mind drifted back to the last time she'd tried to run. She'd made it to France. To the airport. And then someone had grabbed her from behind and dragged her into a corner. They'd beat her bloody, drained her of blood nearly to death, and carted her back to Nathanial. To her master.

He hated her. He had stopped using her sexually, but he never let go of his pets. Never.

At least she was off limits to everyone else.

Tears drowned her eyes before overflowing down her cheeks. She had to get information out of that man. It was time to up the stakes again.

The next morning Emmy opened the heavy door with grim resolution. She walked in with her usual calm indifference and selected the heavy whip from the back of the rack. She let the cool leather slide through her hand and then fall to the floor. The soft sound had the man glancing back. His gaze touched her weapon of choice before he turned back. She thought she heard a huff of derision.

I realize I didn't hurt you with the other whip. I won't make the same mistake this time.

His large broad back showed the welts and wounds from yesterday. They scored his back in angry red marks. Crossing to his front, to stand directly in front of him, she looked down at his defined chest. It had the same welts and wounds, already starting to heal. He was a large, robust man with heavy cords of muscle. He knelt as he had for the last three days and didn't complain once. He didn't shift. He didn't try to get more blood to his legs. He endured.

This was a man who endured.

His gaze rose to meet hers, unflinchingly. Strength and power burned in his eyes. Also a knowledge in himself and a viciousness that made her knees weaken and her hand tighten on her whip. He'd be trouble if he challenged her. She'd fight him as best she could, but if he were free, she didn't have much faith she'd be left alive. He'd charge through the slices of her whip and break her neck. It'd be over in moments.

"I need answers." Her voice sounded unnaturally loud in the drafty space.

His gaze traveled over her face and lingered on the blue

and purple bruise covering her eye and cheek. It drifted down her body next, but not sexually. He noticed her stance and posture before his eyes glued to her side. To where Nathanial had kicked her and cracked a rib. Thank the gods she got her mother's fast healing or she wouldn't have been able to complete their session today.

"I've mostly taken it easy on you. But you are out of time. I will accept your name first, of course. Do you wish to give it?"

That burning gaze locked with hers for a moment. It delved into her with raw force. And then turned away toward the wall. Waiting for what came next.

So she gave it. Hard. With all her experience, and all her knowledge, she railed on him with one hit after the other. The crack of the whip cut through the air. Slices opened up on his body. Blood started oozing from his wounds.

"Name," she demanded.

He stared straight ahead.

She hit him harder. Slashed at him. Tore his skin.

His face went pale. The muscles on his substantial body flexed. When she switched to his back, she could see his arms straining. Even his feet were flexed against the pain.

"Give me your name, and you can end this," she said between slashes.

She walked to his front, again. His gaze swiveled up to hers. Defiance etched his every feature.

"You force my hand," she whispered.

He held her eyes this time. She flicked her whip with a practiced hand. An experienced hand. The tip ripped away flesh. Flayed him. Stripped him of flesh piece by piece.

Most men would've passed out by now.

She gave him another. And another.

His eyes started to dull. The fire within them doused. A shadow crossed over his features and his shoulders sagged. It wasn't the pain that was doing this, though. His mind was dwelling on something. Something in his life, or his past, was taking his attention. He'd done the same thing yesterday—he'd battled some sort of inner turmoil.

She kept at it, harder now. The memory of Nathanial's forced touches bled into her consciousness. The degradation of being passed around to random people and exposing her vein ate away her thoughts.

She hit him even harder as tears worked their way up. He *had* to submit to her. He had to give her *something*. She couldn't take going back to that life. Not again. She'd climbed out of there. She'd made herself their torturer. She'd earned her independence!

"Give me your name!" she seethed.

A lost look washed over the man's features. A haunted, broken look entered his eyes. With the next strip of the whip his lips curved downward, but his body didn't slump. He was fighting it. Fighting whatever hurt more than this whip. Whatever ate him from the inside out.

Damned if she didn't know that from experience.

Without meaning to, her punishment eased. Seeing his features, his dejected loss, his battle with something only he knew, sent shivers through her. Reminded her of what she faced on a daily basis. Of the expressions she so often saw in the mirror when she held the razor blade and dared herself to cut her artery.

In the next instant, it all cleared. His inner-battle ended. His eyes snapped open with wild hunger. The hard light of triumph burned deeply. His whole body straightened and flexed. A huge display of muscle rolled and moved. His large manhood sprang upwards, tenting his sweats. His eyes delved into hers again with an invitation.

No, not an invitation. An appeal to share in this moment. To join with him.

And then it occurred to her. Like a flash of awareness, she finally *saw*.

She couldn't break someone that was already broken. That had been done for her. And while he could triumph over the pain, he hadn't been able to build himself back up. His experiences had broken him, but no one had reshaped him into a whole being again.

She'd been wasting her time. She needed to move to the next step: compassion. She needed to treat him like she'd already torn him down, and now make him into what she needed. Her slave.

But how did she move on to the next step without an open line of communication? Usually she'd gotten answers before she tore the men down. She could then build on those answers when she reshaped them. How could she reshape when she wasn't the one who broke him?

Kindness? Honesty?

"I'm not really sure what to do with you," she started. She hung up her whip and bent to the bowl of water and sponge in the corner. A moan slipped out as her rib screamed in pain. She straightened up with effort and took a moment to collect herself before taking a few steps and kneeling carefully at his back.

"You are not responding as you should." She gently laid the sponge against his back. He flinched, but didn't try to twist away. Slowly and methodically, she began to clean him up. "I'm going to have to try some new techniques before they try and pry you open with magic. They know, though, that magic tends to kill eight times out of ten. You could probably withstand it, but it is a terrible way to get information. The subjects are incoherent afterwards. It's usually used for punishment or their horrible amusements."

She straightened up again, desperately trying to ignore the throbbing pain in her side. She crossed in front of him and kneeled. Her eyes found his, and paused. He looked back with an assessing type of stare. Trying to figure her out, maybe? Trying to figure out why she suddenly changed tactics?

She leaned forward a small bit, waiting for him to spit at her. Or try to bite her. Or head butt her. Really any number of defense mechanisms men resorted to after extreme doses of pain from someone they originally wanted to have sex with.

Nothing came. Just that beautiful, tranquil stare of a man who had confronted his demons and came out on top. It was commendable, but she bet his demons were ghosts. She had those, too. They gave her nightmares. But the real demons in her life weren't dead and buried. They haunted her in the flesh. And parceled her out as food for punishment. And beat her when she didn't live up to impossible expectations.

Yeah, let him try to triumph over her demons. *Then we'd see if you're as tough as you think you are.*

She dipped the sponge into the murky red water and gently applied it to his torso. "I will win, you know. I see that you are pitting yourself against me. Will versus will. I will win because I have to."

She glanced up to find his eyes studying her still. His intelligence and strength shone through. Made the brown of his eyes vivid and entrancing.

She'd once found Nathanial's eyes beautiful, too. What a mistake that had been. A mistake that, once made, could never be unmade.

She went back to her cleaning in silence. When she was done, she put the sponge back in the bowl and lifted her gaze to his. Determination and compassion looked out at her. Also, if she wasn't mistaken, confusion.

Being honest befuddled him, did it?

She smirked and stood, hardening her features so the pain

in her body didn't show. She stowed the bowl and prepared to leave. She needed to think about how to open him up. How to get him to talk. She had today. If she didn't get something by the end of today, she'd take her chances on the run. She had to. There were no other options.

"Why the outfit?"

Emmy jerked to a stop with her hand on the door handle. It took her a second to place the deep, gruff voice as coming from the subject. She couldn't help the look of shock as she turned to him.

He didn't repeat himself. He waited patiently while staring straight ahead.

This was on his terms. He was asking a question, not giving an answer. He was trying to assume control.

She should ask his name and, when she didn't get it, walk out. Then she should resume her next cycle later in the day after she came up with a plan. That's what she *should* do.

Nathanial's threat sounded in her ears. His smug, sneering face swam in her vision.

Taking a deep breath, she walked around to the front of him. His gaze lifted until it found hers. He glanced at her outfit poignantly before resettling on her gaze.

"Do you not like women?" she countered, bracing her hands on her hips and bending enough to pronounce her cleavage.

The man huffed and minutely shook his head. He looked back at the wall.

A thrill of fear washed through Emmy. She couldn't lose him!

Her mind raced before she settled, once again, on honesty. What else did she have? "Men are aroused by this outfit. It sets them up for failure."

His gaze once again rose to hers. "How?"

"When men see a sexual object, they assume the woman is presenting herself to be taken. By him, of course. They delude themselves into thinking they are her master. That they are in control because their penis says they should be. Then I hurt them. My violence against them is seen as a violation of their desires—a traitorous act. Rage takes over. But they are bound. They aren't in control. They spiral into a form of madness, thus breaking themselves down for me. I just help the process."

The man snorted. "Then you only come in contact with weak men."

"That formula doesn't work on everyone, but it works on most. It cuts down my labor."

"And pain works on the rest."

"Usually."

He paused for a moment before asking, "Were you punished because I didn't speak?"

Tension tightened up Emmy's body. She glanced at the door; she should go. She was breaking the rules of a torturer. She'd given him power, and now she was letting down her guard. Letting him into her life.

Slippery slope, Emmy. You are walking a very slippery slope with this one.

She glanced at the door again.

"I'll take that as a yes," the man said in a low growl. "Did you fight back?"

Without meaning to, and unable to help the defensiveness, she answered, "Do you fight back when your boss punishes you? Your leader?"

"No. Because usually I fucked up and knew it was coming."

"I see. And if you didn't mess up? If you didn't know it was coming?"

His jaw clenched and unclenched. "I've never had violence

pushed on me from a superior without due cause. If I did, I would fight back."

"And you would probably be killed."

"Probably."

"I would be killed. Without question. Or subjected to something worse. I'd rather take the punishment." Emmy snapped her mouth shut when she'd realized what she'd said. How much she'd said.

"Anyway," she said in a brusque tone. "You'll see more of me, now. Things need to progress. I will no longer stop when you've had your epiphany. I'll continue on until you can't hold your head up. We'll see if prolonged pain will loosen your lips."

"It won't." His gaze was on her again. "I'm not afraid of pain. I'm used to it. What questions do you need answers to?"

Emmy's eyebrows furled. In response, he smirked and said, "I don't have any great secrets. I'm sure Sasha, my mage, is trying to find me right now. She's probably getting with her white mage teacher and coming up with some nasty spells that will tear this place apart. All they have to do is find this place. And she will, eventually. Or the Boss will. Or those mongrels will. Or all those strange humans will. It's only a matter of time. As long as you have me, dead or alive, they'll come for me. You're on the wrong side, sweet cheeks. You sound American, mostly, and you almost look human with your stature—you don't need to be hanging around with no group of Europeans. They haven't gotten with the times."

"Sasha is the human?" Emmy asked with a firm voice. "She's allowed to be mage?"

The man's eyes burned into hers. "They don't treat you great here, huh? You're human, then?"

She raised her chin, not quite sure how he could read her so easily. "Half. My father. I was mostly raised in America. That's why I have this accent."

"We just got a halvsie. More useful, straddling that line. Didn't much like him at first, and I used to hate humans. But they grow on you when you get to know 'em. Kind of a gentler species until they get riled up. Humans, that is. Not the halvsie. He's a nut."

Emmy couldn't stop herself from smiling. She turned away to hide it. "What's your name?"

"Jonas. I guard the mage. Don't bother asking me any questions about her. I won't answer. But you can know whatever you like about me."

"All on your terms, huh?" she asked, facing him again once her features were schooled.

He shrugged his large shoulders. "You're trying. This is out of your hands. Like I said—I'm used to pain. I'll take it right to the grave. Almost have many times. And you're great with that whip. Too bad you're so stuck up or I—"

His mouth snapped shut before he finished his thought. His gaze once again hit that back wall.

Unable to help her curiosity, she said, "Finish."

He smirked. "That's just it. I'd like to finish. With you. But that shit makes you uncomfortable."

Anxiety rolled through Emmy's insides. Before she'd made the conscious thought, she was walking toward the door. Before she'd left, she heard, "See?"

He was right. It did. Her only experience had been years and years of being forced. There'd been nothing she could do. No one she could appeal to for help. No rights, and no way to fight back. She'd just as soon never be touched by a man ever again.

But she had the stranger talking. Jonas, his name was. She had him talking, and she had some information for Nathanial. Nothing too substantial yet, but as long as something was coming, they'd think she was doing her job.

Now she just had to figure out how to build him up in her

image. To make him want to give her everything. About the mage and whatever else Nathanial wanted to know. She had to appeal to Jonas' soft side—because she knew he had one. Helping her, studying her, inquiring about her wounds—yes, he had one. He was a hard man with a soft core. She had to appeal to that softness. But how?

And then she knew. There was one woman who would charm any man. She'd worked her way into this compound by batting her eyes and swinging her hips. She'd taken blood from all the top members—men and women who rarely gave anyone a taste. She was now one of Nathanial's favorites and often shared his bed.

Emmy walked to the back of the first floor and took the stairs up two flights. There she turned right and walked until the end. She knocked softly at the door. A moment later it opened with a swirl of air and perfume. The beautiful woman stood framed by the door, one hip jutted to the side and her perfect breasts pushed forward. Her flowing red dress was shimmery and see-through.

"Oh, it's you. What do you want?" the woman asked.

"Hi Darla. I wondered if you had a moment?"

CHAPTER FOUR

Jonas heard the door open slowly behind him. His stomach filled with butterflies. Something about that beautiful little female had him anticipating seeing her again. There was something in her eyes. A strange sort of vulnerability that had him wanting to protect her. He'd never experienced this before and he had no idea what to make of it.

Maybe it was because she held him captive. This room, his numb legs, the treatment—that was probably it. He was most likely responding to her as a captive would.

Whatever. He kind of liked this. He just wished she wasn't so shy of males.

A flash of anger had him balling his fists remembering the scared and disgusted look in her eyes when he'd mentioned sex. Someone had screwed her up. That was pretty clear. Someone in this place. Probably the same asshole who punished her instead of worked with her. Hell, when they were trying to get information out of that shifter, the Boss never held Toa responsible for his failed attempts. Instead, he'd worked with the blond-headed idiot. Tried to come up with something that could bring the captive around.

"Jonas."

The word was like honey poured across his body. She came around him slowly dressed in a shimmery red dress that was all but see-through. The usual graceful sway of her hips and assurance in her step was absent, though. Instead, her hands were held rigidly at her sides. Jarring movements and uncomfortable shifting dried up all the sex in the room.

"If you're trying to seduce me to make me an idiot, I'd prefer the whip," Jonas said.

She glanced down at her body in confusion before slowly walking toward him. Her smile didn't reach her eyes. She lowered herself to kneel directly in front of him. Her sweet breath fell across his face. Her baby-blue eyes held his. A small crease formed between her eyebrows, giving her away.

"You got to this part too soon," Jonas helped. "You're supposed to wander around and show off your wares. Then, when I'm salivating, you're supposed to slink forward. Maybe put your groin in my face or something. Then kneel. Then tease me. When I beg, that's when you ask questions or whatever it is you want. You got here too quick."

Anger flashed in her eyes.

"Plus, you still look uncomfortable," Jonas continued. "If you can't pull off a cleavage show, how are you gonna pull off near-nakedness? What are you going for, anyway? Love via my dick, or something? I said I'd answer your questions."

Her mouth turned into a hard line before she abruptly stood. "Fine. How about this." She stalked back to the corner and came back with a wooden paddle. "Want pain? No problem."

With only a small grimace from what must've been the pain in her side, she leaned down, swung her paddle back, and delivered him one hell of a blow. The slap hit off his wounds from earlier and spread the pain across his chest. Aching bites tore into him as the wounds, barely knitting together, all broke open. He sucked a breath in through his teeth.

"Hurts, huh?" she taunted. "How about this?" She hit him again. Then once more, pounding him with the blunt object with such violence he had an instant hard-on.

"Again," he breathed, falling into it.

He felt another solid slap. And another. She was taking out her aggression on him, but doing it with an air of precision he hadn't had before. The landing of each blow was well-placed for maximum effect. She'd chosen the paddle so she could beat the hell out of him without rendering him unconscious or killing him. And she stood over him with a mastery and dominance that set him on fire.

"Again," he repeated.

The blows stopped. His erection throbbed. He opened his eyes to find her staring down at him with a crooked smile. "You're on my time. You'll get punishment when I say you get punishment. And right now, I need an answer or two before I take you higher."

Jonas' mouth dropped open as his dick gave a lurch. His ardor rose. His eyes traveled her beautiful face and then dropped down to her perfect body. Great gods he wanted her. This strong, dominant woman who was so full of pain and loathing for her life that she didn't realize the strength she possessed. He could help her—bring out the wild vixen in her. And, in turn, she could quell his beasts. She could take control while he happily lost it.

She'd just figured out his weakness. His real desires. Now the test of wills began.

"Take me higher? Sexually, you mean?" Jonas countered, trying to back her down.

The shadow passed over her eyes for a moment, but a glimmer came back in immediately. "I mean to beat the living hell out of you. And you'll like it. And you'll beg for completion. And if you do what I ask, I'll free one of your hands for a time so you can take care of it."

"It will be you who takes care of it. With your body. Or your mouth."

A crease formed in her eyebrows as she wrestled with something internal. Anger flashed again. "I don't give a crap how you take the pain, Jonas. You want to get off on it, what is that to me? Nothing. But the only person that is going to be fucking you is yourself. In the meantime, you'll tell me everything I want to hear. Starting now."

He almost flinched as she rushed him in the heat of passion. Violence and aggression poured from her body. She slammed him with the paddle two more times before crossing to his back and hitting him three times there. He soaked in the pain. He let it swirl around him. He let it fire him up and then pool in the base of his cock. His past didn't rear up, this time. The taunts didn't come. The remembrance of lonely days or constant torture didn't surface. All he could think was her and the moment. Her mad plight to use him to extinguish her rage.

"Touch me," Jonas groaned as his body lit on fire from the inside out. "Please. Turn your pain into pleasure with me."

The paddle didn't return. She walked around to the front of him with hard eyes. "Does the human mage know Cato? Is it true he backed her?"

Jonas' head was swirling. His cock was so hard he couldn't think. She stepped closer, dousing him in body heat. Her breasts, barely visible, were so close. If she leaned down he could suckle them through her sheer dress. "Please."

Her hand came up and slapped him across the face. "Does Cato back the leader of your clan?"

He opened his eyes and connected to her burning gaze. Passion boiled there. Not sexual, not yet, but something else. Wild abandon. A fighter crouched. A caged animal paced.

"I will not answer questions about the mage or the Boss."

She kneeled in front of him slowly. Her soft hands trailed up his arms and to his shoulders. She glanced down between them. Following her gaze, he saw his dick straining out to her. He almost leaned forward to try and kiss her. To feel those full lips as she lost herself to ecstasy. But when her eyes came back up, that familiar haunt was there. That fear. That inadequacy.

It really ruined the mood she'd just created.

"Can I get a conjugal visit?" he asked as he squeezed his eyes shut to try and ignore the pounding in his erection.

"Damn. I'm no good at this charming guys thing."

He felt the absence of body heat. The sudden cold made him shiver.

And then the paddle again. She'd figured out how to torture him after all.

Emmy slammed the door shut behind her, had a quick glance around to make sure she was alone in her room, and then threw herself onto her bed. She'd just left Jonas. Finally walked away when he was panting and blustering to hold her. Not touch her, not make love to her, but *hold* her. He kept saying, "Let me share your pain." Or, "Let me help you turn your pain into pleasure."

It should've been gross. It should've disgusted her. But her body was on fire. Her stomach was butterflies. Her core was throbbing.

She'd never felt like this before. And while she'd tortured hundreds of people, it'd never been like that. She'd felt *free* somehow. She'd put all her fear and hatred of her life into those strikes and felt released when he moaned in pleasure.

She put her hands out in front of her and stared at them.

Then she hopped off her bed and stared at herself in the mirror. The same girl stared back, except for the eyes. There was a vivacity in the eyes she'd never seen before. They were now the eyes of a stranger, sparkling away.

Whose smile was that?

She kind of wanted to touch him. Just to see. With him tied up, and no way to force her, she just kind of... wanted to see if... it was still a disgusting act when she was in complete control. She wanted to see how his face changed when she gave in and gave him the touch he so ardently desired.

Shivers erupted across her body. Which was a decided improvement over her usually roiling stomach with the disgust of thinking about sex.

One thing was for sure, though—she had to get out of here. Jonas was a bit crazy, but he was not like the men in this compound. Or in their compound in England. He didn't hate humans, for one. Their clan—as he called it—accepted them. Lived among them. Human women were having their babies, and that was not considered an abomination. She wouldn't be considered an abomination!

She crossed to her desk and opened a drawer. As she reached in for a map, her door swung open. Nathanial entered the room, followed by Luc, an unwashed piece of trash that constantly sneered at her in disgust. Except when Nathanial was handing out her blood, that was. Then he was first in line.

Her heart sank.

"I got answers," Emmy said in a rush. "Cato has backed the leaders—the mage is the mate and co-leader of Stefan. Stefan is the one they call the Boss."

Nathanial stared at her with ice in his gaze. "I see. And how did you manage to get this information?"

"I've worked my way in. He's hard to pry information out of, but I am cracking him."

"Yes. I can see the triumph in your eyes." Nathanial glanced down her front. She couldn't help the flinch when she remembered what she was wearing, but she didn't cover up. He'd exploit that weakness just for fun. "I had heard you asked Darla how to charm a man. And that worked, it seems."

"To a point. I haven't touched him, but he would like me to."

"I see." Nathanial glanced at Luc. "Get out. She will get no punishment today."

Emmy couldn't help the sigh. Nor the uncontrollable shaking under the glare of Luc as he trudged from the room.

"I will be allowing Darla an attempt with him later tonight. It appears she knows this man, who is called Jonas. She was in his compound with him. She had to flee when attempts to get rid of the human mage were thwarted by the human-animals. Commendable, however, that she tried. Anyway, she says she has some affinity with this Jonas. And, of course, she is... persuasive."

Something within Emmy tightened up. "Give me another try. I am confident I can get something out of him."

A small smile graced Nathanial's bloodless lips. "Yes, you do have pride in your work. That is one of your commendable qualities, of course. But we will allow her a session, I think. Since she already knows him, and he seems to respond to sexual advances over pain, I think she is a better bet."

A tightness formed in her chest she didn't understand. Within Nathanial's stare, though, she didn't have time to dissect. "Yes, sir."

Close to dawn Emmy couldn't help pacing through her small quarters. She'd heard Darla made alterations to the room where they kept Jonas. She'd put in a wide but comfortable chair, and a long cot. Obviously she was going to try and have sex with him. That horrible creature would have sex with anything—Jonas was just her next target.

It shouldn't matter. If she got him hard, and then finished the deed, it shouldn't matter.

Darla had had an hour so far. And with her track record, she'd surely been with Jonas before. She knew his desires. And his kinks. She most likely knew what got him off and what made him crazy—Emmy had figured it out in a couple days, so after growing up together, Darla would probably have a blueprint. She'd get information out of him easily.

Would she make him as hard as I did earlier? Would he beg to help take her pain?

"Doesn't matter," Emmy said to the empty room.

Something irritated her about the whole thing, though. Regardless if she wanted to admit it or not, she'd shown Jonas her vulnerability, and then she'd shared her suffering. She'd given him a glimpse into her so she could have a larger glimpse into him. And that had left a mark. It had connected them in intimacy.

"Doesn't matter," she said again. Her voice sounded dead in the silent room.

Emmy started to pace again. Jonas' eyes filtered into her memory. Focused and entrancing, he always looked at her with equal parts respect and knowing. Like he could read her. Like he cared about her suffering in this place. Like he understood her trials.

"It does matter."

She was striding out of her room a moment later.

No one had ever offered to help shoulder her burden. No one had tried to back off when they saw she was uncomfortable. And she didn't share intimacy with anyone.

Not anyone.

That connection she had with a perfect stranger, forged in

a high-stakes situation, was more real than any she had in her life. She'd had a conversation with him—something she didn't even do in her day-to-day life since she had no friends. And he didn't care about her half-half status. He didn't care that part of her was human.

Men like him were worth protecting. She just had no idea how she was going to do that and live another day.

"So, the fates have led you right back to me, huh?" Darla paced across the stone floor in her red high heels and see-through gown. She'd always had a great body—toned but curvy—and an even better face. She'd also always been a raging bitch. Jonas hated her. He had no idea how the Boss had always dealt with her.

"And now Nathanial knows I have *all* sorts of insider information about the Boss and his stupid human mage. All *sorts*. What the interior of the mansion looks like, how he operates, how the Watch goes about their business—even the connection you have with the shifters. Pretty soon, you won't be needed at all."

"I wonder why he didn't talk about his business with you before now? Didn't trust his pretty piece of ass, huh?" Jonas deflected as he stared at the wall. Three huge males had muscled him across the floor and into a chair. There they'd attached the chains on his arms to the wall above his head and his legs to a metal hook. He now faced the door whereas before he was facing away. It was a new vantage point. Plenty of new cracks to look at to pass the time.

"He's got a lot of clout in England," Darla was droning on. "He's only in America because of the destruction of the Council. As soon as he can, he's going to step in and assume control."

"That didn't answer my question. Also, I can't imagine your new fuck-friend would be thrilled you're giving me that information."

Darla scoffed and shimmied closer. "You think he'll trade you? He won't trade you. He's going to kill you just as soon as he has all he needs. Who are you going to tell?"

"For a female who can't seem to complete any sort of organized plan to her benefit, you sure are certain of future events."

Darla ran one fingertip across his cheek. She traced the curve of his lips. "How active is that Cato person? Is he moving around much? Are there many at the Council worth worrying about?"

"Go away, Darla. You're annoying."

"Is that right?"

Jonas felt the hard bite of her nail digging into his face, followed by a trickle of blood.

"I seem to remember you like pain, is that right? That's what turns you on?" She bent. A warm tongue licked up his cheek and played over the wound she'd just given him. "Hmmm. You taste good. I want to suck on you as I ride you. Make up for all those years that you ignored me."

"Takes a lot to knock down your confidence, huh? Constant rejection wasn't enough—now you're going to force yourself on me. Well, bad news is, it doesn't work like that for a male. I gotta be turned on for you to ride me. And that ain't gonna happen."

"No?" Darla did a slow walk over to the wall with all the tools. He could see her fingertips glide across the various instruments before curling around a leather paddle. She took it down and turned with a sultry smile. "I know how to play the Dom. You just never gave me a chance to prove it."

"Does your new squeeze know all you planned to do was screw me? That you didn't intend on getting information?"

"I'll get information. I'm a good lay." Darla stopped in front of him, drew the paddle back, and *whacked* him across the chest. The effect was a light stinging where she'd disturbed the older wounds. She took aim and hit him again. Then again.

If possible, she was even more annoying while trying to be in control than when she was just sashaying around.

"Or maybe..." She pulled his sweats away from his waist to expose his dick. Then, bending over, she yanked them down until they gathered around his ankles. With a chilly hand, she clasped his limp shaft and started stroking. "Maybe a knife would be faster. Or a mouth..."

Gracefully, she fell to her knees and bent over him. He felt the warm wetness of a mouth circle his tip. Ordinarily, yes, that would be enough to get the ball rolling. With her, though, this wasn't gonna play. There was no way he'd give her the satisfaction.

Jonas called up memories from his youth. Of the taunts and the laughter. He picked hers out and focused.

What a little shrimp. You'll never have a mate. No female will ever want such a puny little nothing. Look everyone—a female *is bigger than him!*

Her beautiful face had been screwed up with disgust as she'd pointed and laughed at him. All his classmates had joined in.

"Impotent, huh?" Darla asked in a mocking voice.

"With you? Yes."

She scoffed. "Is that right..." She hiked up her dress to her waist and threw one long leg over his lap. She settled her nude sex on top of his.

"You can't get a male hard—how do you still think you're desirable?" Jonas pulled his head back to get as far away from her as possible. He just barely saw the door swing open, but couldn't see who came in.

"I have four co-leaders in this clan treating me like their mate. Four. And one is a woman," Darla explained with pride as she moved her hips in a circle over his. Her warm wetness slid across him as her face dipped to his neck. "I'm good at what I do. Get hard for me, baby. I've always wanted to try you out. So gruff and manly. I bet you fuck real smooth, though. It was always rumored that you did. Deep and sensual. Everyone wanted to give you a try, but you're so selective. Why is that?"

She sucked at the base of his neck as she gyrated forward on his manhood. The friction would've had him standing on end, but the woman rocking over him shriveled his desire. His cock stayed limp.

Jonas felt the pinch of her teeth when he heard, "I don't think that's working, Darla."

The honeyed pleasure of that voice dribbled down Jonas' back. The protective instinct he heard in her feminine tones had his heart pounding. He wanted to run into battle with her. He wanted to stand by her side as they took on a wall of enemy and triumphed. She needed that. She needed a way to fight back and overcome whatever was keeping her down.

"What do you want?" Darla asked in a hiss as Jonas' sweet torturer sauntered forward. She still wore that nearly see-through gown, but she might've been in battle garb for all she noticed. Her eyes were burning and a whip was thrown nonchalantly over her shoulder.

"I want you out. Draining him isn't going to help. I can still get useful information out of him."

Darla turned back to Jonas. She surveyed his neck. "And you will—as soon as I finish with him."

A whip cracked. Darla screamed and scrambled off of Jonas. She arched her back and reached around to touch it as she twirled toward Jonas' torturer. A neat slice was cut down Darla's smooth skin. Blood was already starting to trickle out.

"You just made a big mistake, *human*." Darla glared at the younger, shorter female. "You interrupted my interrogation and enacted violence on the superior race. And I'll make sure I'm the first one who gets a taste from your neck, right before you're passed to the under-workers. Won't that be nice? Having filthy hands reaching between your legs and into your body as their stinking breath falls on you? Making the rounds and delivering yourself for their bite? Oh yes, I'll make sure Nathanial makes you pay for this."

Jonas' torturer lifted her chin in defiance, but Jonas could see the rigidity in her body posture. He noticed the trembling lower lip and shaking hands. With a firm voice, though, she said, "I'm his pet. He doesn't allow anyone to touch me but him. You can parcel out my blood—that's nothing new. But after that, you're just a pet, too. You don't have *half* the power you think you do."

"Is that right?" Darla's voice dropped an octave as she stalked toward the other woman. "I wouldn't be so sure, *human*."

As she passed, Darla slapped the other female. Jonas' torturer's face whipped back. She staggered into the wall as Darla opened the door. Jonas stood in a rush, his body going taut. His need to fight fired into him. His hands were now bent behind him painfully, though.

Before she left, Darla shot him a glance. "We aren't done yet." The door shut in a heavy slide.

"That wasn't wise," Jonas said to his torturer. "She's a vindictive bitch. She'll do everything in her power to make you suffer."

The female shrugged. "It's all I know. Suffering, that is. What's one more enemy? They can fight over my punishment."

"That's what they do, then? Treat you like a pet?" Jonas

asked softly as the female crossed to her stand of tools and replaced her whip with badly shaking hands.

"Pets at least want to be kept. Usually. I'm not a pet. I'm a slave. I'm used for my body or my blood. Humans can be released into the wild—as Nathanial says—but I'm an abomination. I'm half and half. Nathanial doesn't want any of his kind announcing themselves to the humans before he has control over the Council. He wants to plan how the humans find out about your kind."

It finally became clear what was going on here. What the foreigners really wanted. "They want to see what the humans will do when confronted with another species. They want to see if they can dominate," Jonas whispered. "What fools."

"And when the humans freak out—which they will—this compound will probably run right back home. You all will be hunted, and they'll be nice and safe in hiding."

"They know where the Mansion is." Adrenaline was coursing through Jonas' body. "They know where the shifters are. Probably know where the other clans are around the country, too. If the humans are excited enough, and they are looking, they'll eventually start noticing us. And then..."

"And then they'll realize you don't get diseases. AIDS doesn't affect you. They might think you have the cure to cancer. Most of you will be killed outright. And the rest will end up in labs. Yeah. Nathanial is thorough. He's done his homework. I'm pretty sure he knows the outcome, but the powers-that-be wanted to see if the modern age would allow for more open-mindedness. But he'll totally ruin what you guys have going."

"The Boss will cut his feet out from under him. He won't get a chance to set this in motion."

The female sighed and leaned her head against the wall. "He's an excellent magic worker, Nathanial. One of the best in the world. Your people will never find this place. They could be standing right on top of it and they wouldn't see it. That's why he was elected to head up this project. He's not the oldest, but he's the best. And the most ruthless."

Jonas stared at the female huddled near the wall. "Why are you telling me this? Why have you been so honest with me?"

She shrugged and turned so her back was flat against the wall. She looked away from him. "You've been nice to me. You're a prisoner, whom I've beat beyond the tolerance of all but a few, and still you've cared about my... issues."

"Issues." Jonas snorted. "Such a human word. Sasha uses that all the time." He sobered and sat back down. He felt the tug of the cuffs on his wrist. Felt the raw skin on his ankles. He needed to get out. He needed to warn his clan—to get Dominicous and Cato active. This Nathanial might be great, but Jonas bet he was nothing compared to Cato. And if so, he was nothing compared to Cato with the help of Sasha and her following of humans.

"Why are you still here if you're treated how you say you're treated? And what's your name? You never said."

The female glanced over at him. "Emmy. My name is Emmy. And I've escaped before. I'm actually pretty good at escaping. And hiding. But I have some sort of magic tag on me, I think. I'm always found. And they always bring me right back."

"Well, it's a sad day when I'm the nicest person you know." Jonas tugged at the chain again. There was no way he was pulling this out of the wall. He glanced back up at the female. "So what do you plan to do? Turn me on some more, not touch me, and then wait for them to kill me and pass you around? That your plan of action? Because if it is, that's a piss-poor plan of action."

"I have at least a day to get more answers out of you. They need more information on the Council. You were there

—you still have use. And if you have use, I have use. We have a little time."

Jonas shook his head and yanked at the chains again. Anger pinged through his body. He called the elements and tried to work a pure shot of fire. He directed the stream into the metal at his wrists. A moment later, he felt the bands heat. Next, his skin started to sizzle.

"What the hell are you doing?" Emmy asked as she hurried toward him. He immediately felt cooling relief as Emmy reached over him and laid her hands on his cuffs. She leaned back so she could look down on his face. "I sure hope your mage is better than you at magic."

"Thanks," Jonas said gruffly. "I'm not great with spells. Not those kind, anyway. Most of my magic is for fighting."

Silence descended as she stood over him, looking down. Her heat fell around his body. Her smell, floral and feminine, curled around his senses. He remembered her burning eyes and how she'd handled that whip aggressively. And he remembered how she gently washed the blood from his body. Hard and controlling one minutes, soft and caring the next.

He let his head fall back so he could look up into her beautiful, haunted blue eyes. "It worked."

"What worked?" she whispered. Her sweet breath dusted his eyelashes.

"Your methods. You've succeeded."

"No. I didn't. The goal is to make the prisoner attached while remaining unaffected. I failed."

Her gaze drifted across his face and dipped down to his mouth. "I've never had a good experience with men. It's always only been Nathanial. I've never been in control. I think it's why I'm so good at this job—I get to stay in control. I'm always the master of the room."

"When things get too wild, and my aggression climbs too high, I often need someone with a firm hand to level me back out. To put me back in line. I need someone to take the control away so I don't lose myself to violence."

A ghost of a smile graced her red, full lips. "Yin and Yang."

"Let me touch you, Emmy. Please. I'll be gentle. I won't touch you anywhere you say is forbidden. You can zap me with magic if you get nervous."

"No, I can't. I can't do much with my magic, actually."

Jonas could hardly think with the pounding in his cock. With the warmth of this beautiful, dainty female above him. With the desire to feel her soft skin on his body. "Why?" he asked in a whimsical voice.

"I told you. I'm an abomination. My magic is human. They wouldn't train me."

"I can free you of this life, Emmy. I can take you back with me, tracker or no. Sasha will be able to get you free of whatever magic holds you, and if she can't do it in time, the Boss will eagerly await these dirty Europeans. If they come to us, we won't have to bother going to them."

Her little hand drifted through the air. It landed softly on his shoulder. A shot of electrical current blasted through his body. He couldn't help his moan.

"You didn't get hard for Darla," she said quietly. "She was all over you—and she's... *her*—and you didn't get hard."

"She's a bitch."

That hand lightly rubbed across his shoulder and up his neck. Her thumb lightly traced the stubble on his jaw. Delicious shivers racked his body. "She said you were selective."

"I don't have time for idiots."

"You're hard right now."

Jonas gulped. "Yes. Very. You're driving me crazy. Which I get. Don't get me wrong, but—"

Emmy bent toward him. Her face came down slowly. He stayed perfectly still as she let her lips trail across his. His eyes drifted closed, savoring that sweet touch. Feeling the blissful current that vibrated through his lips and down through his body.

"Do you always need to be hit?" she murmured against his mouth.

"Apparently not."

He could feel her lips curl up into a smile before she bent forward and deepened the kiss. He opened his mouth to her, allowing her to slip her tongue inside and playfully explore. Letting her take the lead. She tasted like apples and sage. Her hands slipped down his shoulders and across his chest. Warmth radiated on his skin. Tingles spread across his flesh.

"I will get you out of here, somehow," she whispered as she backed up. "Tomorrow. I'll get you out."

"What about you?"

"I'll... figure it out."

"No." His harsh voice filled the room. "We'll get out together. Call the Boss. No, call Sasha. She's damn pushy when she's riled up. Call her, tell her where we are, and give her the situation. When they show up, we can make our way out."

"I don't have a phone. I don't have any connection with the outside world."

Jonas stared up at those sorrowful blue eyes. "How have you not gone crazy and killed everyone in your sight?"

A melancholy smile graced her lips. "How? What's a whip against magic? Like I said, they track me down and find me. Nathanial doesn't like his property going missing."

"Nathanial is going to die before this is through. That I will guarantee you," Jonas growled. "Not one of these buggers is escaping without answering for this."

"You're sweet."

"Not really. Actually... not at all. I'm an asshole. But a determined asshole."

She laughed and slowly, hesitantly, lowered onto his lap. "I shouldn't do this."

"Please do that," Jonas begged.

Her warm body covered him. Her arms snaked around his neck. "The first time I leaned close to you, I expected you to spit on me. Or bite me or something. Usually that's the first line of defense when a man's hands are tied."

"Hmm." Jonas leaned forward and captured her lips. He groaned when she moved further up his lap. The warmth between her legs rested on his erection. Only a mostly sheer piece of fabric separated them.

"You haven't been like anyone I've ever met."

"Usually that's a good thing." He deepened the kiss. Needing more of her. Taking whatever she would give him. Knowing she had to do this at her own pace, and really liking that that pace was a fast one. She was part his race, after all.

She half-stood above him while staying bent over so their lips continued to touch. She hiked her dress to her waist. "Here goes nothin'," she murmured.

She sat down slowly. Her hands on his shoulders were shaking. Her breath hitched and caught in her throat. Her eyebrows dipped. Fear crept into her eyes as she backed up to connect with his gaze.

"Don't do this if you don't want to. Males will always beg and plead—it doesn't mean you have to give in."

He'd coaxed that small smile again. Her body sat down ever so slowly. Her wetness touched his hot tip. Fire erupted through his body. "Oh fuck."

She kept going down. His manhood slipped past her folds and slowly, painfully slowly, entered her tight, hot sheath.

"Oh—" His eyes rolled back in his head. His heart hammered, pounding on his ribs. He couldn't seem to get enough breath. His whole body was tight, desperate for more. For all of her.

"Are you okay?" he asked through a tight throat. His

whole body was flexed. All he wanted to do was thrust upward and then explode. He didn't have long. The first time with this female and he'd turn out to be a one-pump chump.

He hoped she didn't tell anyone. Charles would never let him live that down.

"Yes. Surprisingly... very okay," she said softly as she started to move. Her hips rocked forward and back. Forward and back. The friction was pounding pleasure into his body. Nothing but pleasure. No residual pain. No stingy cuts or throbbing, aching areas. Just pure, sweet pleasure.

I don't remember feeling this good. Why does she feel this good?

"I can't—" He braced himself with everything he had. Tried to hold back. Tried to hold on.

"I can't—" He gritted his teeth. He clenched his butt.

She rose up a little, and then sat back down. That one, hard pump was all it took.

He exploded. An orgasm rocked his whole body. He shuddered under her, emptying himself. Small explosions of fire burst across his skin right before he turned to jelly. Every muscle in his body relaxed.

"Okay, I can get ready again. This isn't a problem. Give me a moment," Jonas panted.

He opened his eyes to the largest smile he'd yet seen. Her eyes glittered.

"Don't make fun of me—that's not fair." He sounded like a chick. Oh yeah—if Charles ever got wind of this, Jonas would be a laughing-stock. "You've been building me up. I'm better than this. Just give me a second."

"It's flattering," she laughed. She started moving again, slowly. Her hips went around in a circle one way, and then back the next. She leaned forward and captured his lips as she rocked forward.

"That's a nice way of saying it's embarrassing for me," Jonas grumbled. He could already feel his body responding, though. Her unsure movements, her experimental rising and falling, and her teasing kissing were enough to be hot and endearing at the same time. She was completely naïve when it came to sex. Completely raw and eager to experiment with this new control.

He wouldn't allow himself to dwell on why that was. Not until he was standing over this Nathanial male with a glowing orange sword in hand. Instead, he put his head back and fell into the sensations of her movements. Her gorgeous body rocking over him. Her bouncing, rising up until she was at his tip, and then slamming back down. Not only was he rock hard again, he was ready to release round two.

"You're making a mockery of me," he panted, eyes squeezed shut again. "Let me touch you. Let me help you get there."

"No need," she panted. She rose up and sat down again. And again. She struck up a rhythm. Each sit-down was harder and harder. The friction built as he plunged in and out of her. He couldn't help lifting off the chair now, rising to meet her fall. Pushing into her with all the strength he could muster in his position.

"Yes, Jonas," she exalted. She tilted her head back with a smile. "*Yes!* More!"

Their bodies slapped together. She bent back to him with a deep kiss as he moved inside of her. The pressure increased.

"Oh Jonas," she sighed. Her insides gripped him. So tight. So hot.

He—had—to—

He blasted into her for the second time. Thankfully, she shook over him a moment later. Her insides milked him, contracting even tighter around his shaft.

"YES!" she yelled.

Her body collapsed over him. Her arms draped across his shoulders and her face was nestled up against his neck.

"You can take my blood, if you want," he said softly. "I've never let a female do it before, but you can. If you want."

He felt her smile against his skin. "I've never taken blood before. Maybe next time. Baby steps."

"There has to be a next time, Emmy. We shouldn't wait. We need to get out, now."

Her body straightened up. Seriousness took over her gaze. "If I let you free—even if I showed you the way out—I can't do the invisible charm. And even if I could, they know how to undo it. You'd be dead before you took two steps toward freedom."

"We need the Boss and Sasha. You know this place, Emmy. *Think.*"

He saw her vision cloud over. A worry-knot formed between her eyebrows. "I have one trick—*one* trick—I can do. My mom showed me before they moved her to another compound. My magic is weird—it's not like hers—so when I tried the thing she showed me, it turned into something else. I only have one time, though. Nathanial will learn it and disable it after just using it once near him. I can get a phone that way, but... how fast can your friends get here?"

"How close are we to the Mansion? To Pine Hills?"

Tears swam in Emmy's eyes as she slowly shook her head. "Probably fifty miles."

Relief washed through Jonas. "That's fine. It's been a few days. They'll probably have some vague idea where this place is, by now. We just have to hope they're close. And don't worry about your human magic—they'll be able to teach you. There are already a bunch of batty humans learning in the Mansion."

A tear overflowed. "It sounds like a dream."

"Well, we have to get out of here, first. And that won't be too fun." Which was an understatement. It sounded impossible.

CHAPTER FIVE

Emmy's body was luxuriously relaxed as she wound her way to her room. She'd expected to have a panic attack or something. Or maybe just go numb with memories. But it hadn't been anything like that. What started as kind of an impulse became the best experience of her life.

But now came the hard part. Jonas was her salvation—she knew that as well as she knew her own name—but they were trapped in this festering pool of disease. Security was much more relaxed at home than in his compound. On enemy soil—as Nathanial thought of it—he wasn't taking any chances. She knew this, because to make that map of hers, she had to test all the entrance and exit points. Even the "secret" entrance to this place had guards. She could slip out, but getting the prisoner out? It didn't look good.

She pushed open the door to her room with her map in mind as she caught the familiar presence. Nathanial sat at her desk as he had the other night. One ankle was crossed over a knee and his fingers were intertwined. Shivers wracked her body. This was his "faux patience" stance. It meant she was in trouble and would be punished.

"Hi Nathanial." She walked right up to him. She'd hoped to think about a plan, maybe wait that day after all. Not with that edge to his eye, though. She didn't have a day.

She didn't have an hour.

"Emmy. I am absolutely heartbroken. Darla tells me you interrupted her interrogation. Being the dear-heart she is, she tried not to fault you, but I couldn't help but see the whip mark. You scored one of your betters while defying one of my direct orders. This grieves me."

"She wasn't interrogating him. She was trying to screw and bite him." Emmy felt the magic run through her body.

"Now, now. You know I dislike when you are vulgar. Well. You will be glad to hear that your prickly charge is no longer needed. Darla has produced someone who used to work right beside Cato. He is quite well connected. Pity I didn't hear of him before now. But you know how it is—so many want to join our cause, I don't have time to speak to them all. Luckily, however, Darla had. She was quite the find."

"Great."

"You will not be pleased to hear, however, that you must be punished. And Darla is right—having a human pet for so long does look bad. We'd hate to have others think I favor your kind. So you will go into the higher level of humans distributed for good deeds. I will choose who gets you intimately, of course—while I applaud her foresight, I still do not like sharing. Your blood, however—that can be distributed more openly. Others will need the boost to their magic level. We will take the Council premises soon."

"Why do you keep me, Nathanial? If you hate me so much, and hate my kind, why do I need to be under your thumb? No one else forces humans—or anyone else. Why me?"

His head tilted at her words. "You are a remarkably pretty girl. And there is a certain allure in lying with one such as yourself. I often wondered if you would get with child. Humans seem to find that easier. Three-fourths of my race means the offspring is likely to have my type of magic. This would ensure I could raise my child as my own. There was always the chance it would have human magic, and that I would have to abandon it, but it was worth the risk. Unfortunately, you are barren. And since you lack sexual finesse, I found that there was no use to you."

"Then why keep me? Why not let me go?" she pleaded.

"Because what if *I* was the barren one? I couldn't allow you to bear someone else's spawn. Then I would be ridiculed. And yes, now we have that problem, which is why I will be sure to choose those who are infertile. If I choose wrongly, and you do get with child—well, there are ways to rectify that."

White-hot rage burned through Emmy. Red hazed her vision. Anger clouded her judgment. Without a second thought, she reached forward and placed her hand on Nathanial's neck. A perplexed expression crossed his face, but he did not flinch. That would be a sign of weakness for an advance from a human. She'd counted on that.

Before he could shock her with magic, she dumped her special spell into his skin. Fire and ice rolled, heating and then freezing his skin. His throat swelled. Red bled into his face. His eyes bulged as his hands flew up to his throat.

"Fuck you, Nathanial." She dumped him out of the chair as he worked at the spell. She snatched his phone out of his pocket and ran. Sprinted through the halls. She'd hide with Jonas for as long as possible and hope someone showed up to storm the place. If not... well, Nathanial would find her eventually, and she'd deal with it then.

As she ran, she typed in the number Jonas made her remember.

"Cato, we're en route. I can't move any faster than I am." I looked at Stefan with a suffering look as we sat in the back-seat of Jameson's car. I thought driving the extremely fast and gloriously scary Ferrari was the better way to travel, but not one person sided with me. I suspected Charles had mentioned that I'd gotten air when I took it out the other day to relieve some stress. He was such a scaredy-cat with speed.

"I know, Sasha. And I truly am sorry for calling every five minutes, but you know how it is when you are waiting—each minute stretches. I will say, however—do I have time for a quick chat?"

"Cato…" I ground my teeth. The man acted like a child sometimes. He was losing his marbles, that was clear. "Yes. You have time. We are still in the car headed to you."

"Oh yes—how silly of me. I get thinking about the battle to come and forget the details. Where was I—oh yes, I am really pleased that your network of humans has proved so useful. I did know that Rudy disappeared into this area of the world, but I couldn't pinpoint where. Then your spies and your witches—you have really come through."

"But you said you can't see the building."

"Yes, that is true. But once you get here we will try some spells and see what lands. I have every reason to suspect the London faction sent Nathanial. He is an old… acquaintance of mine, and exemplary with magic. He can do things even I have not seen."

"Not encouraging, Cato," I said in dry tones. I rubbed my palm across my forehead to try and dislodge the worry. Cato had mentioned more than once that we were going up against an old, excellent, experienced army of fighters and magic-workers both. They were the best, and had been waging war with those close to them for hundreds of years. I'd been in my profession less than two years. So the experience levels were a bit skewed on my side of things.

"Not to worry, Sasha. Toa tells me you have handled the basic link with him very well. You keep up excellently, and when put under pressure, come up with exciting and terrifying spells. I can't wait to wage war at your side."

Goodie.

"How long do you think it'll take to break the concealment spell, Cato?" I asked.

"Oh, probably a day or two. That little Delilah-human is coming, correct? I hear she is just great at picking apart very intricate spells. Quite the marvel for one unused to magic and with such a low power level."

"Yes, she is, but she's heavily pregnant." She'd nearly caused a riot at the Farm when she said she was coming to help. Putting pregnant women in harm's way wasn't something Stefan's people did. Well, it wasn't something most people did, but Stefan's people got really violent about it. Her mate tried to challenge Stefan. Charles and Paulie had to subdue him.

"Yes, we will guard her, assuredly. Now, Sasha, how are your two little ones? I would so love to meet them. You must—"

My phone beeped with call waiting. Glancing at the number wasn't helpful since I didn't know it. And while usually I wouldn't answer, to get Cato off the phone, I'd make exceptions. "Cato, I have an important call coming through. Can I talk to you later?"

"Yes, of course. Of course. Are you any closer?"

"Bye, Cato." I clicked the button to end the call and answer the other with an extravagant eye-roll. "Hello?"

"You're supposed to say who you are," Charles "helped" from the front seat. He was trying to take over for Jonas in the business etiquette department and succeeded in making me want to beat him senseless.

"Sasha?" a harried female voice panted into the phone.

"Yes, this is *Sasha*—see Charles, I didn't need to say my name."

"If you did, you would've saved that person asking," Charles retorted.

"Sasha, this is Emmy. You don't know me. But I am the person who has Jonas. Kind of."

I bolted forward in my seat and waved at Jameson to quit talking to Stefan. "Where is he? Is he okay?"

"He's—yes. He's okay. For now. I'm—it's a long story. I'm trying to get him out. I just took down my... jailor, basically. The guy that keeps me here. He'll be looking for me. And they will kill Jonas when they find him. But I can't get out of here with him. Or, at all, now. They'll see me. I'm not allowed outside. Um. This is jumbled. Sorry. Just—I can tell you how to find this place. But you have to come quick. We don't have much time. And even still, we'll have to sneak out when you bombard this place. There's no other way to get out alive."

"Will you keep this phone on you? I can trace this phone."

"Ask if it's a trap!" Charles hollered. Stefan was staring at me, wondering if he should take the phone and handle this. I wasn't great at organization.

"Can you put Jonas on?" I asked in a choking voice.

"Yes. Later. But now, please write this down. I'll tell you how to break the spell—I'll try, anyway. How close are you?"

"Half hour. We'll be there in a half hour. We already have people waiting to get started."

I heard a relieved sigh and a "thank God." After that I scribbled frantically on an ad in a magazine Charles was able to scrounge up in Jameson's car. It was clear Emmy didn't know much about magic. She spit out words and sentences that sounded like a second-hand rant from a mad scientist. I wrote it all down, though, hoping Cato would be able to make sense of it. After that I heard a heavy door open and a low hum that sounded vaguely like Jonas.

My breath caught. My knuckles turned white where they clutched the phone. And then I heard, "Sasha?"

"Oh my God, Jonas!" I couldn't help a racking sob. "Are you okay? Did they hurt you?"

"Yeah. I liked it. Where are you?"

"You would—"

"What's his status? He take down half the guards yet, or what?" Charles interrupted in a rush.

"Can he get out?" Stefan asked.

"We're on the way," I said. "Twenty minutes, now. Cato is already there. Sounds like Rudy is somewhere in there. Cato's worried they are going after the Council."

"Yeah. They are. This crew is up to no good. They're trying to take over."

I heard what sounded like heavy metal clinking. Hinges creaked.

"Ah. That feels good," Jonas sighed.

"What? What happened?"

"Emmy released my hands."

"How were you holding the phone?"

"Shoulder. Sasha, listen, do you know how to take off a bit of magic for tracking somebody?"

My mind raced. I'd never even heard about the ability to do that. "I'm sure Toa would. Or—wait—Cato totally does! He was talking about how he was keeping tabs on Rudy. That was probably how. I could ask and call you back."

"Is it something I'd be able to do, though?"

My heart sank. Jonas wasn't great with spells that didn't involve violence. Take down an army with his hands? Yes he could. Do a simple tripwire spell that a red could do? Nope. That wasn't his specialty. "Probably not."

"Thought not. That's fine. I'll figure it out. Just do me a favor."

"Anything."

"Make a huge bang when you get here. Make some sort of huge distraction. By the look on Emmy's face, we're going to need it."

"Just one more thing, Jonas," I said softly. "Are you sure we can trust this girl? I mean… she switched sides pretty quick."

"She's half human. They treat her worse than a farm animal. She has a shit life, and she's coming back with me to start over. We can trust her."

She's coming back with you? A human? "Okay."

"And one more thing," Jonas said in a deep growl.

"Uh huh. Wait—are you into this girl? A human?" I couldn't help but ask. Who was this guy all of a sudden?

"She's hot. Listen, that bitch Darla is here. She's working the top tier of people and they are buying whatever she is selling. Just thought you'd want to know."

"That bitch!" I yelled. "I am going to punch her in the mouth. Seriously. Will she never fuck off?"

"Who?" Charles leaned toward me.

"Your lady-love, Darla," I snarled. "All right, Jonas, go hide. Stay safe. You'll hear me when I show up."

"Sounds good. And Sasha…"

"Yeah?" I didn't want to hang up. I didn't want to disconnect with his voice. I was terrified this was the last time I'd talk to him.

"Thanks for coming. Knew I could count on you."

"Of course. Of course I would," I said with a shaking voice.

"Now. Chin up. Get tough. Show 'em how big your balls are. Emmy and I'll be waitin'."

The line went dead. I stared at the phone for a moment in

sorrow and bewilderment, both. "What is his fascination with my lady balls?"

"What's his status?" Stefan asked in a low tone. His dark eyes bored into mine. "What are we going into?"

"We're up against some old Europeans with some excellent magic skills and who don't treat humans very well. I think it's safe to say they won't be using any humans. Cato's smart. He had me build up the human magic so as to entwine it with his. Two sides of magic going against one. That has to count for something."

"We have the home turf, too, Sasha. Don't forget that. Playing-field advantage." Charles stared out the windshield. "I wonder if they'll use shifters, though."

"Probably. They used those shifters to scout us out." I chewed on my lip in thought. "But they weren't as organized as Tim. I think we definitely have an advantage. The question is, can we combat against their superior magic-working. We might have more strength, but they might have better spells."

"Cato knows what he's about." Stefan shifted in his seat. His demeanor was calm even though his eyes were on fire. He was mentally preparing for a battle he had no doubt he would win. "He's been at this a long time. Plus, Dominicous has organized a front line from all over the country. They've been preparing for this ever since the Council fiasco. We're ready."

I wished I had his confidence. Jonas' life was on the line.

CHAPTER SIX

Jonas shook out his hands and stood in a rush. He swung his body around and rolled his shoulders. Being stiff was the worst thing for what was coming. He'd be dead before he ever got in motion.

He pulled up his sweats and tucked the phone in the pocket as Emmy hustled back to the rack of tools and took down two whips. She tied them around her waist and bent to the ground. Digging her fingers in the cracks, she worried one stone from the rest, revealing a small hole. Moving quickly and with fantastic economy, she pulled out a belt of knives. Working under the whips, she attached the lethal belt over her hips, overlaying her sheer gown.

"You are probably the hottest warrior I've ever seen," Jonas said.

Emmy looked up with furrowed eyebrows. The worry cleared from her face for a brief, red-cheeked smile before she went back to her occupation. "We don't have long. We need to get out of here."

"Do you have a sword?" Jonas glanced at the wall of tools behind her. A paddle wouldn't do much good against anything sharp, and he wasn't about to go twirling a whip in public. That was something chicks did.

Emmy glanced behind her and refocused on him. Worry clouded her gaze. "No. I was never taught how to properly use one, so I've never kept one around."

Jonas shrugged and stalked toward the door. "I'll take someone's off them. How long have we got before your captives come calling?"

Emmy replaced the stone and straightened up. She wiped her hands on her dress and retied her whips. "Any time. I caught Nathanial off-guard, but he would've unraveled my spell nearly immediately. He doesn't think I can go far, so he's probably not hurrying, but still..."

"We just have to stall." Jonas couldn't help moving toward her and gently putting his hands on her shoulders comfortingly. He felt her flinch lightly at the personal touch, but she didn't shrug him off. "Sasha will get this bitch humming. If anyone can shake it up, it'll be her. We just have to stall long enough for her to get pissed, and then make our escape."

"She's not as close as Nathanial, and my directions were probably not very helpful."

Jonas moved his hand up to her face slowly. He touched her cheek as their gazes held. In a soft, reassuring voice, he said, "She'll find a way in, and she'll blow this bitch sky-high. I have the best mage on this planet because she is a true survivor. And I have the best leader, who will run circles around Nathanial. We just have to stall. Show me around this place, and I'll keep it lively until reinforcements come."

Tears glossed over Emmy's eyes. One stray tear released and wobbled down her cheek before he wiped it away with his thumb. He bent, slowly, and lightly touched his lips to hers. He felt her hands wrap around his middle.

"Some warrior," she said in a low tone. "I'm scared shitless."

"That's just because you're thinking about it. C'mon." He kissed her harder before stepping away. With a quick jerk, he swung open the door and prepared to rush a crowd of males with swords.

The dingy hallway waited, sleepy and empty.

He smirked back at her. "See? So far so good."

"You don't feel pain, and you're not afraid of anything. What are you, Superman?" Emmy tiptoed around him on silent feet and peered to the right. A few bare bulbs dimly lit the old, stone hallway.

"I'm Superman's kryptonite."

Emmy huffed and took off at a jog to the left. "Well keep up. I assume you can run."

"When I have to. I don't make a sport out of it, or anything."

"This is a serious maze down here. They mapped it out a long, *long* time ago, but very few people ever come down here. I bet I'm the only one that really knows how to get around."

"What did this place used to be? Why is it here?"

Emmy shrugged as she turned left into a dark maw. She slowed to a fast walk. "I got the human affinity for the light, so I don't have great night vision. Bear with me. Anyway, this was built by the Europeans a long time ago, I think. Like, first settlers era. Your race, obviously. To hide from the human settlers and whatever else. I think this below area was the dungeons, and then all the stuff above is for living. The stuff above has seen a lot of makeovers, but down here—well, who cares about prisoners, right?"

"And you've spent a lot of time in this place?"

They turned left and then right. Only one bulb every twenty yards lit their way, now. The darkness encroached on Jonas' visibility, blurring the once-sharp lines. Emmy spread one hand in front of her, and one to the side, lightly skimming the wall with her fingers and hesitantly advancing. She probably couldn't see much at all.

"I go where Nathanial goes," she explained in a hush. "He visits this place once every couple years to check in with... whoever. People spying at the Council, mostly. I often acquire a captive, and spend the rest of my time wandering down here. Solitude is better than sneers or belittling. Hence my knowledge of the tunnels."

"I take it you found one of the maps."

"Yup. It was in the library. I took that, and a map of the surroundings. I have an American passport, so the idea was to eventually get free and disappear."

"How'd you get—" Jonas cut off as Emmy stopped in a drafty, dark void. She reached back blindly, groping for him. He took her cold hand and immediately threaded his fingers into hers. Electricity surged up through his arm and coursed through his body. An erection sprang to life, begging him to pull her onto his body. Instead, he took a deep breath and finished his sentence. "—a passport."

"I'm not afraid of your contact. I figured I'd be scared of all males for... a great long time. It's nice to know I'm not as screwed up as I thought I was."

"That makes one of us."

Emmy huffed and started walking at a right diagonal. "Can you see better than me?"

"Rough outlines."

"Okay. Well, there is a tiny hole up here that leads into a different tunnel. I think someone must've gotten lost up here once upon a time and blasted their way through. It wasn't on the map."

"Secret tunnel?" Jonas saw a rough wall reaching to either side of them. The very faint light from a bulb distantly behind them lighted on the pockmarked and jagged stone that should've met at a corner. The hole was somewhat oblong and made a divot in the ceiling. "Never mind."

"My dad was American and a doctor. He made up a birth certificate and got me a passport. It's outdated, but... I'm a citizen."

"What happened to him? Your dad?" They inched along five feet of pitch black. Jonas was as blind as Emmy was until they stepped around a corner and another distant light softly glowed down the corridor.

"Disappeared. He was here most of the time I was—he lived in the area, I think. He wasn't a prisoner, or anything. I think he loved my mother. But soon after he gave me the passport he... stopped coming here. My mom was transferred out. I haven't seen her since, either. Nathanial cut me off."

"What's the story with that guy? Why the obsession with you?"

Jonas could feel her hand trembling in his, but she kept silent. If she knew, she wasn't willing to share. He could respect that, but he couldn't stop a kernel of rage burning at what this monster had done to her life.

"Okay, just here." They walked into a little alcove, followed a circular corridor away to the left, and found a shadowed door. If she hadn't led Jonas directly to it, he wouldn't have seen it. Not with the way it seemed to crouch in the shadows within the wall. A squeal of metal saw the heavy door swinging into a dark space. Standing at the doorway, there was no way to see how big the room was, its shape, or how deep it went. Given the nature of the corridor, though, chances were the room was round.

Emmy took two steps in, stopped, and sidestepped to the right. "Close the door behind you, then do as I just did. We'll be blind, so you'll need to walk around my traps."

"What kind of traps?" Jonas asked as he pulled the door

shut behind them. The click of the latch sounded unnaturally loud. Like he'd just shut them into a tomb.

"Just furniture positioned in the way. Enough to slow someone down so I could go at them with my whips."

"But... you'd be trapped in here. What would be the point? Magic could take you out."

"There's a tiny door in the back. If we get a chance to run, we won't be going the way we came. Nathanial will follow me with whatever tracking thing he has. That'll take him in a straight line. He can't get here in a straight line. This place was designed to keep prisoners in. If they tried to escape they'd be hopelessly running around the inside of this place. It'll buy us time. Hopefully... it'll buy us enough time."

Emmy led them blindly through a series of steps, not unlike an elaborate dance routine, around the room. When she got to a place she deemed their goal, she stopped, about-faced, and sat down slowly. The creak of wood echoed around the stone room. Jonas followed suit, sitting right beside her on what felt like an old bench. This time the creak was more of a squeal. He paused.

"It should hold," Emmy whispered.

"How do you know?"

"I don't. But it sounded comforting."

Jonas huffed and resumed. The bench wobbled, but held. "Okay. Now... we wait. I'm already bored."

Silence descended on them like a heavy, suffocating blanket. Stagnant air prickled Jonas' skin with implications. With what he knew was coming. He was sitting here, without a sword, with a woman he'd grown to really like, while warriors wielding buckets of magic wormed their way toward them.

He wasn't good at this. This waiting for a battle to come to him. He wasn't built for it.

"Is there room to pace in this place?" he asked in a gravelly whisper.

He felt movement next to him. Emmy took her hand from his grasp. It reappeared on his chest and slid up to his face. Her palm, strangely soft even though she worked with her tools, cupped his chin. "I can distract you."

The bench groaned as she shifted her weight. Another little palm slid across his thigh and cupped his erection. He closed his eyes, since they weren't any good here anyway, and let her pull his head toward her. He felt lips touch the side of his mouth lightly before repositioning fully on his. Her mouth opened, inviting him in.

He turned to her and gathered her into his lap. The feel of her, touching her—it was an exquisite sort of heaven. The electricity they'd known before exploded with the increased contact. He deepened their kiss and squeezed her body close. "Do I need to be gentle?"

"If you don't want to break the bench."

"No, I mean... are you worried about not being completely in control?"

"I am in control. If I asked you to stop, you'd stop. Immediately. I know that. I trust you."

Jonas stood with her before setting her down on her feet and repositioning her body. He then pulled her with him to the hard stone floor, cold to the touch, and sat her on his lap. "So we don't break that bench."

Emmy laughed. A low, throaty sound that vibrated his bones. He put his arms around her and just held her for a moment, liking the feel of her delicate body against his. Liking that she curled up within his embrace and rested her face against his neck.

"Your problems have lived with you all your life," Jonas said in a low hum. "Until today. I give you my word that soon they'll be your past. And we can face that past with a smile and a sword. Or a whip. Soon all this will just be memories."

"What about your past? What is it that haunts you? That

makes you need to feel and own the pain until you come out blazing yet tranquil?"

"You're way too eloquent for the likes of me—I should point that out. I'll never hear the end of it from Charles. He'll say it's a green card situation." Jonas gave a low chuckle. The darkness and hush of the room swallowed it up. "I was a runt when I was a kid. A tiny thing. Smaller than everyone. People thought I was deformed. Or that I was human. I didn't have a firm grasp on my magic, which developed late, like the rest of me, and I couldn't fight with any sort of strength. I was made fun of ruthlessly. My mom left me—which really is just not done—and my adopted father, who took pity on me, died a few years after the adoption. I was alone for most of my childhood—no friends, no respect, and no peers."

"How did that change?"

Jonas ran his fingers through her silky hair. "I had a huge growth spurt. I packed on muscle, got a dose of magic, and nearly overnight became a giant. I'd practiced my sword work and offensive magic religiously because of the bullying, but it hadn't been much good without strength and power. As soon as I got that strength and power..."

"You kicked ass."

"Yes. Lots of ass. I earned a lot of notice, but didn't accept it. Not from those people who'd been kicking me when I was down. I eventually met a couple guys that had lost parents in the same incident I did. They were a bit older, but ruthless. They had their own shit. We developed a sort of respect for each other, and then bonded. The three of us earned a name, and then we helped the strongest and smartest of us to become leader."

"And he's still leader."

"Yes. One of the best. They want him for Regional, but he just became a father, so he's putting elevated duties on hold."

"And he's mated to the mage? The human?"

"Yes. I hated her at first—you should know that. I hated that she was a human. After being taunted and ridiculed as being human half my life, and starting to believe it... Well, I wasn't eager to accept her. Human, to me, was a dirty thing. A *lesser* species. Small and weak—helpless—like I was when I was a kid. Her presence brought back painful memories."

"And she changed your mind? How?"

Jonas' fingers stilled as he thought back. He remembered, very clearly, Sasha's determination to learn her magic. Her fearlessness. Her valor. And, most importantly, her willingness to run into battle when she could've gone and hid. "She didn't act like how I'd always heard humans acted. Like her sissy boyfriend at the time. Or other humans I'd run across. She had traits I admired. She was small, weak, untrained—yet she didn't hide from bigger enemies like I had when I was younger. She always rose to the challenge and ran at danger. She didn't need a growth spurt or a bunch of muscle to find her courage. She just goes for it. How can you not respect that? How can you not want to fight beside it?"

His fingers resumed stroking. "And then there was that halvsie she found. That guy—he's a nutcase. Most people, besides the Boss or Jameson, won't look me straight in the eye. Not for any period of time, anyway. He did. Right when I first met him he shot me a hard challenge. Couldn't give a shit if he was outgunned or not. And just like Sasha, that guy threw his balls to the walls immediately. Waltzed into a larger race with a hard eye and infallible confidence. He's my kind of nut.

"Then there's the other humans—those harebrained witches—and babies being introduced, and more magic... Cato's right. He's the craziest of all, but he saw it from the first moment of meeting Sasha. Looked beyond all our prejudices and saw what would make the race as a whole stronger. And we are—we *are* stronger as a united force." Jonas shrugged. "Just got to open the eyes to see it. Gotta swallow that pill."

Emmy slid up his chest until her lips slid across his. "Then I got lucky with the timing. Touch me, Jonas."

Jonas wasted no time. With his fingers splayed, he slid his hands down her smooth back. He deepened the kiss, tasting her. Feeling her tongue retreat and invite him in. He moved his hands to the top of her back again, and this time when he slid them down, he hooked his thumb in her straps and pulled her gown down. Her warm chest met his, skin on skin. He could feel her hard nipples rubbing against his pecs.

After removing her whips and knives, he brought his hands around her waist and pushed them up her stomach and over her firm breasts. She moaned into his mouth as her body moved away from his, giving him space to work. He did so. He bent his head and kissed down her neck and onto her chest. He flicked a nipple with his tongue and pinched the other before enveloping the small bud with his hot mouth. Her moan was louder this time. Her hips gyrated against his, needy. Insistent.

He increased the suction on one nipple before moving to the next. Then more suction, bordering on painful. He just wanted to see her tolerance. See what she liked. Her sharp inhale of breath was followed by a groan of delight. He bit softly before backing off and blowing lightly.

"Oh holy hell," she breathed.

Jonas flicked her nipple again, manipulating it with his tongue. He let his fingertips drift down her back in light caresses. Teasing her. Making her anticipate. When her breath started to increase in heaviness, and her hips started to swing wildly, he sucked in her nipple and bit a little harder this time. He pinched the other with the same strength.

"Oh shi—" Her body trembled against him. Her hands clawed at his back and her head fell to the side. "Oh wow."

Jonas started to kiss up her neck again, light and teasing. Building her again softly. Making her wait for the harder friction. Learning her body with touch in the process.

"Take my blood." Her voice was heady. Somewhat wild. "You'll need the strength."

"So will you," he countered. He nibbled her lips.

"Not as much as you, Jonas." She rose up onto her knees. He leaned forward and found her breasts. He sucked one in as he felt hands at his waistline. "Help."

With a smile, he lifted up on his hands so she could work his sweats down around his thighs. He sat back down on the cold, stone floor. A rug of some sort would've been nice, but as her body moved over him, and her wetness touched off his tip, he forgot all about it. Instead, all his focus went to the hotness of her core as she sat. Her core enveloped him. Electricity filled his body. The world dimmed to just her. To the feel of her body and the subtle movements over him.

"Take my blood," she urged with a sigh. "I want it."

He couldn't deny her. Not when she asked like that, with her voice desperate. Wild. Needing to feel this thing between them with reckless abandon. She rose and then sat down on him again, harder. As he plunged into her, feeling sensations he could barely handle, he bit the delicate skin on her neck. She rose up slowly, breathing heavily. He sucked in her essence, taking a long draw.

"Oh my—Oh gods. Oh—" Emmy clutched onto him. Her nails dug deeply into his back and then scored down his skin. Hot, stinging pain flared. Then pooled. Then turned into white-hot pleasure.

He thrust upward into her as she was coming down. His skin smacked off of hers as pleasure assaulted him. Her blood fell over his tongue in a burst of flavors and colors he'd never tasted before. Like a deep, underground river, the currents arrested him and sucked him under. Her floral scent wrapped around him as he tasted spices and danger. The desire to run headfirst into battle rose up. Of courage and steadfastness. Of hot nights and victory. His blood sang as it mingled with hers. His adrenaline keyed up.

He couldn't think any more. There were only sensations. There was only her.

"You taste—" He took another long draw. Her moaning filled his ears. Her body moved faster over him. His manhood plunged in and out of her. Her body stroked him. Made his balls tingle. Made his head swim.

His eyes rolled into the back of his head as an orgasm tore through him. She shuddered over him a moment later, crying out and then muffling it within his neck. Their panting filled the quiet room. Her presence, her body, her feel, filled his everything.

They would live through this, and he would make her his mate. There was no other way to play it.

As that thought settled into him with a comfortable surety, they heard distant shouting.

"He's coming," Emmy said in a strangled voice.

CHAPTER SEVEN

I hopped out of the car a moment after it rolled to a stop. We'd arrived in a dusty field ten miles outside of town. It was the only place in this area that didn't have some sort of farming setup. With the yellowed grasses and uncultivated ground, it looked like a farmer had long since given up and moved away, never having sold his land so someone else could make a go out of it.

Once upon a time, I wouldn't have noticed. I would've just passed this field with a brief glance at the deserted nature of it. Now, however, I rolled my eyes and scoffed. *Obviously* there was something hidden here. No way would land this fertile go unworked. No way would one building-size plot of land, perfectly square with the perimeter defined, *not* be housing a bunch of Stefan's race trying to hide from the humans.

A line of cars had stopped in the middle of the street. Many had pulled to the side, ruining some cabbage, but a great many had just stopped. If someone wanted to get through, they were out of luck. I had no idea what Cato had done to keep the humans away, but whatever it was, it worked like Raid to ants. Not one person drove down this road that wasn't here for a huge battle over American soil.

Warriors of one size—gigantic—gathered along the edge of the road. Each body stood straight and tall, dressed in leathers with swords at their sides or on their backs, sporting grim and terrifying expressions. These were the best of the best, that was clear. With their perfectly-sculpted muscles decked out in vicious, jagged scars, these gals and guys had all seen plenty of action. Their shoulders were set and eyes hard, staring at the empty space as if looking into the eyes of their enemy. They were just waiting for someone to kill.

The line of warriors was four deep and as long as the plot of land. There must've been a thousand people for the front line. Behind them, sporadic, were more warriors with less scars but harder expressions. Most looked older, and often they surveyed the toes of the men nearest the dirt. They were probably the commanders who would orchestrate the charge.

Cato stood in the cabbage field. Spread out around him were people with some mark denoting their ability at advanced magic. Some held hands, and some stood with heads bowed, but all stared unfocused. They were working.

"Love." I turned at Stefan's voice. He walked up beside me as he scanned the front line. He glanced back at all his warriors getting out of the cars, then turned his attention down to me. "You don't need me for this. I'll be working with the warriors." He bent so his face was closer and his eyes bored into mine. "Stay safe, do you hear me? Don't be a hero."

"I'm totally going to be a hero." I winked at him. I was pretty sure I still had raging anxiety in my gaze. Before a battle, I was scared shitless. This wasn't new. The fireworks had to actually get started before my courage got fired up and my brain shut off.

"I love you." He bent and kissed me. "I'm leaving Charles

with you. Hopefully we'll have Jonas by our side soon enough."

"I just have to crack this bitch open and let him out," I said with bravado I didn't feel. The magazine paper of directions Emmy had given me crinkled in my fist.

Stefan nodded as warm comfort infused our link. "Call me if you need anything."

I watched him stride away with a sense of loss. That feeling never went away when he put distance between us, and the rush of bliss always rushed me when I saw him again. That's just how it was.

Which was not helping at the moment.

"All right. Time's a wastin'." I glanced back the way we'd come and saw Paulie stalking down the street with his straight and determined walk. My clan nodded to him as he passed, but those that didn't know him gave him a double-take. He looked both human and like Stefan's race, and he wore his halvsie status with pride. Gold flared up his arms, highlighting his tattoos.

A crew of mostly hippies and older women followed him like a flock. They tittered and looked around with wide eyes, many staring at that field as if their gazes would eventually penetrate the magical defenses. If Paulie got double-takes, the witches and warlocks (there were men now, too) got open-mouthed gawks. We had the largest collection of human magic-workers in the entire world. Seriously, the whole world—unless someone was hiding their humans, that was. Cato didn't think so, though. We were an anomaly and often laughed at within the Council.

Of course, being that the Council was a broken-down wreck, and since my clan's united status was producing a larger next generation as well as increasing our magical ranks, we cared not at all. And not only that, Toa said we were finding traits in magic they thought were long extinct. Tarot cards, crystal balls, palms and ghosts acted as a medium for many humans to foresee the future, or work intricate magic that bent the elements in different ways. Toa was setting up a residence within the Mansion so he could spend more time analyzing. He'd come up with some crazy things, mostly forgotten magical relics, working with the rudimentary magic the humans used.

"He hasn't figured out the notes you gave him, obviously," Charles said as we walked toward Cato.

My mouth turned into a thin line. I had hoped that giving Cato the directions over the phone that Emmy had given me would have opened some magical door and we'd arrive to a battle already in progress. Or at least with a gate we could storm. No such luck.

We wound between the cars and slowed as we neared Cato's cluster. He looked up and met my eyes, as if he'd seen me coming even though he'd had his eyes closed. And he probably had, since I was always connected with magic. Just like him.

"Sasha, ah. Lovely to see you. Thank you for those notes. So very helpful." The group around Cato split down the middle, opening a path for me to walk closer.

"Have you made any progress?" I asked, half-turning so I could watch Stefan organizing his men with Dominicous, who stood slightly removed from the waiting warriors.

"We've cleverly masked and then dismantled the spells. They are extremely intricate. The notes have been invaluable, though strangely cryptic."

"I don't think the person who gave me those works with magic. She's half-human. I get the feeling—"

"Ah yes. Emmy, if I am not mistaken. She would be the only one with intimate knowledge of Nathanial's spell-working—who has surely set all this up. He assumes, incorrectly, that humans cannot understand the working of magic. He would be more open around her. No one but him could have. Yes. Emmy has a rare and sought-after blood type. It is like a drug for those going into battle, I have heard. Nathanial guards her religiously, though his treatment of her..." Cato looked out over the cabbage field in thought. "I wonder how she was able to get his phone without being subdued immediately."

"I get the feeling she's into Jonas. Or using him to get out. He seems into her, at any rate. He thinks she has a tracking thing on her person."

Cato nodded slowly as his eyes lost focus. He stared at me without actually staring at me for about thirty seconds. I shifted both in impatience and from being extremely uncomfortable. When his eyes honed back in, he gave me a slight smile. "One more down. Only two to go and then we can start working on the disillusionment charm."

Impatience won out. "Are you serious? Holy crap, Cato, this is taking way too long. Jonas is in there." I glanced around and caught sight of Delilah hobbling up the road. Her man was holding her hand and glaring at everyone around them. Birdie was right beside her with new ink on her arms, a dagger at her back, and dressed in a Karate gi that didn't fit her huge bosom quite right.

"Let's get this show on the road. I'll get all the witches assembled. We're either going to take these down or blow them up." I made a circle in the air with my finger as I connected eyes with Paulie. He nodded and turned to the crowd of humans at his back. With only a head flick, he had them all walking to me with nervous smiles and wringing hands.

This was the first time most of them would see a real

battle. I had a feeling they thought it was like watching Shakespeare in the park. I wasn't planning on spoiling the horrible, shocking surprise of what it would actually be. I needed them here too badly.

"They're like a pack of children," someone said from Cato's crew. I could see a few members of the Clutch, the mages to the Council members, shift uncomfortably. They were supposed to be backing Cato—thinking humans in their fold was a good idea. It didn't seem like they were really onboard with that idea, though.

Didn't matter. We'd prove them wrong. *Hopefully*.

"Delilah, how are you?" I asked, looking worriedly at the heavily-pregnant woman.

She smiled. Irritation ate away at her features, though. She was about ready to pop. "I'm fine if everyone would stop hovering over me. We have a four-wheel drive and know of the closest hospital. I'll be fine."

"Great. Paulie is bringing around your chair. We'll sit you in the back. All we need is to get 90% through the spell, and then we'll get you out of here, okay?"

"Fine, fine." She waved her hand in impatience. "Let's do this."

She was so ready to be done with pregnancy. I knew exactly how she felt.

I ignored outraged murmurs from Cato's crew regarding Delilah's condition as I turned to the humans. Just as I was about to tell them to call the corners—they *insisted* I use that terminology so they could be a little different in their approach than Stefan's people—Toa glided out from between two cars and stopped directly at my side. He glanced over the gathered humans and then honed his unblinking, blue stare on me.

"Sasha, I am having Dominicous and Stefan move

everyone back from the line. We will have them duck behind a line of cars. With that in mind, the magic-workers should push back further into the field. This way, when you don't immediately crack the spell, you can use your method."

My method. Blowing up the spells with my inverted magic. It was another reason having human magic was awesome—no one fortified against us because no one worked with humans. Toa was the leading creator of spells I couldn't just blow away, and that was only because he was tired of me cheating. This Nathanial character wouldn't have thought of it—not with how he viewed humans.

Cheat to win.

"Call the corners, everyone," I commanded as I turned and jogged to the open field.

The witches gathered in a tight horde behind me. Delilah was carried back farther still before her man ran off muttering about moving the car closer. With our mill-in-flocking nature, and the wide eyes and twittering, we were proving how naïve we were to all this. We made Cato's crew look like the military.

Soon that wouldn't matter, though.

I felt the stirring of the elements around me. Like atoms starting to heat up, the swirls of elements raced around excitedly, riding the currents as people drew in power. Toa moved right to my side, his magic ready to link when I was ready. When the witches were ready.

"I thought I was supposed to link with Cato this time," I said in a hush so as not to distract the witches and warlocks. Most of the humans still needed to focus to do this. They'd come a long way in a short amount of time, but they still had a long way to go.

Toa turned his stare to Paulie on my other side, then to Charles in front of me. Finally to all the humans at my back. "You will when we start to battle. For now, as the white more familiar with your... style, I will aid as well as monitor. I will be masking your efforts until your frustration level takes your level-headedness away. Then we will need to plan how you take down their defense."

"Because if I don't do it right, they'll know we're here?" I felt the swell of power behind me. The arms of magic reached, ready to link. I connected with each of them, over thirty in all. Since I only needed their energy, the size of the link didn't matter. That's why Cato and my magic was awesome for this type of thing—limitless power and easy linking, as long as we had the energy to back us.

"Precisely. It would be best to dismantle the traps. After that, faster is better." Toa connected with me and half-staggered. Charles stepped closer and put a hand out to steady him. "They have grown in power, as a whole."

"Yeah. Master Bert has become really good with humans. Who would've known? Okay." I blasted my magic out toward the empty field, and then slowed down. I let the magic descend gently, like a soft mist. Immediately I felt these strange, jagged areas out toward the front. If they were physical, they'd be like clusters of spikes, ready to stick someone who came too close. In addition, there were little feelers. Weird little additions to the spell like tripwires. They were woven tightly within the spell. The whole thing looked like an abstract, beautiful torture device.

I now saw what took so long.

"So... this is intense." I let my magic drift into the cracks and seams, looking at the construction. Finer than any spider's web, and infinitely more sticky; if I didn't work the inverted spell just right, the original spell would go *boom* and spray everyone with sharp, magical spikes. Worse still, it would immediately alert everyone in the invisible complex that we were here.

"Yup. This guy is way out of my league. Delilah?" I didn't

bother glancing back. I could feel her working within my magical touch in that strange way she did.

"I would love to study this. It's... unlike anything I have ever seen," I heard from about thirty feet behind me.

"That's not saying much," Charles muttered. "It's not like she's been doing this for very long."

"Not helping." I rubbed at my brow. "Toa?"

"It took Cato and the Clutch an hour to dismantle the other two. The disillusionment spell is bound to be ten times as intricate. As I understand it, we don't have that kind of time."

"Blow this shit up and let's get in there." Paulie's gruff voice had a few warriors looking back.

"We've been working on the disillusionment charm," Cato said from beside his crew. "Subtly, of course. Just little tweaks and breaks. Getting it ready. If you would be so kind as to sink your human magic in the various pitfalls we have created, as you get a hold of the trap spells, and then apply your adverse magic, I think it will set off the implosion. That is how you are often able to blow things up, if what Toa has said is true. That is why working *with* human power to create spells is the strongest magic known to the world. There is not this imbalance—"

"I get it, I get it," I said distractedly.

"What disrespect!" someone gasped.

It was true, but that guy would talk all day if I let him. We didn't have the time.

"Set it up, Sasha," Toa urged in a low but calm voice.

I really missed Jonas. I really needed him beside me to say, "Nothing to it, human. Let your balls fly and blow this bitch!"

Keeping him in mind, I did as Cato said. I surrounded the traps with my magic and lingered on the detonators. I then led Delilah to the larger structure of magic, a giant spell that covered the whole empty lot like framework. Spells in spells, weaving and winding and swirling around each other. The detail on this spell was so breathtaking, so intense, I just had to stop for a minute and take it in. I wanted to get a feel for it. To let the current, the *flow* of the spell just... shake hands with my magic for a moment. Just taunt me with what was so far above my expertise I couldn't even be jealous.

But I could work toward it. Oh yes. Someday.

With Delilah's help, I let the magic sift inside the cracks. I found the pitfalls and pockmarks Cato had created and planted windings of pure fire. Once done, I nearly pulled out. What I'd planted would work, I was sure of it, but it would come blasting back out at us. That was no good. Plus, I wanted to stay with this spell just a bit longer. I wanted to understand it. To feel it. To internalize it and revel in the mastery of it.

Lingering, I let a piece of myself sink in deep. Sink down to the fiber where even Delilah couldn't go and just hang out for a moment. I let my mind drift, then, thinking of Jonas. Thinking of the best ways to get him out of there. To tear the place apart. To really stick it to these assholes who had come to America to raise hell.

I started shedding spells and ideas of spells and things that might work. I let my magic creep along the floor. I felt the foundations of the building through the cracks and let my magic crawl up through it. I felt people, then, hanging around inside. Standing guard. I felt their magic and their swords. I felt their confidence in their assurance that they were hidden and protected. I felt their vulnerability.

I let fire creep along the floor with me and all around the walls. I planted demons in the dirt and ghosts in the halls, items that would erupt or spin or fog. I planted distractions like Toa had shown me and fire bombs along the roof to let in the sunlight and momentarily blind them.

When I was done, and somewhat at peace and tranquil

with the magic running through me, I felt the hitchhiker. An earth-shatteringly strong white power rode my coattails, tweaking my spells and glossing my attempts. He turned a crude idea into a shining example. He turned a distraction into a crippling pitfall. Cato was taking my ideas and applying his experience to make them better.

"Micro-manager," I said with a huffed smile as I disengaged my mind while leaving all my work behind.

I opened my eyes and then gasped. Cato was standing right in front of me, staring at my face. He wore a serene expression of pride. "You are a marvel, Sasha. What must your life have been that you can so aptly *feel* your way through dire situations? You have displayed a mastery well beyond your years. You and Stefan will take my place, someday. No one will stand in your way."

"Okay, but about the space issue. When you are an inch from my face, it makes me a little uncomfortable..."

"I wasn't about to stop him, Sasha. I'm afraid of what he would do to me," Charles muttered.

Cato's eyes crinkled in mirth. "We will talk about moving you to the Council after this is done. Where are your shifters?"

"Get Delilah out of here," I said behind me as I stepped around Cato. My foot slid off a cabbage plant. My balance jolted off center, having me staggering to the right. Paulie put a hand to my shoulder as Charles put a hand on my head, steadying me.

"My *head,* Charles?" I said as I regained my footing.

"Well? He had your shoulder. I would've grabbed your boob if you weren't all hopped up on magic."

"Yeah, right." Paulie chuckled as we threaded between huge bodies to the center of the street. I found Stefan and Dominicous talking with a few other scary men, who must've been the battle commanders, behind a large van. Tim was standing with him in nothing but a pair of sweats. Ann was to his right in a muumuu. I couldn't help but smile as she turned to me.

"Hi, Ann!" I gave her a hug. "Fancy seeing you here."

With effort, the corners of her lips dipped down into a grimace. Her eyebrows fluttered like a vaudeville act until they finally furrowed into a comical-looking grimace. "I'm supposed to be serious."

"Oh. Sorry." I grimaced back at her. "Better?"

Her eyes sparkled and a smile threatened to break free again.

"Sasha, what is the situation?" Dominicous asked with a firm voice.

I turned to a wall of muscle and glowing tattoos. Every single commander had flares of burnished gold. These six people were packing power. Except for Tim, who turned into a huge, angry bear that could swipe heads off with nasty five-inch claws.

I gulped and inched away. I wanted to go back with the mages again.

"Where are we with magic?" Stefan asked. His comforting presence pulsing through the link again.

"We're going to try and implode their spells. It's all set up." I turned to Tim. "Get your people furry and in place."

"That's my job, Sasha," Dominicous said quietly. Even though his face was grim, I could see a sparkling of pride in his eyes. Also a warning.

I gulped again. I hated it when these guys were territorial. It was like walking in on a pride of lions when they were feasting on a kill.

I ticked the air. "Yes. Right. Okay. Then we just need the go-ahead that you are all in position and we'll blow this place.

They'll be stunned. Hopefully. Their first line of defense probably won't know what the hell is going on. In addition, I've—we've—left some spells that should create some fierce holes in their building. You shouldn't have any problem getting in. You should also have the element of surprise. It seems like, to me, they were really confident in their disguise."

Dominicous nodded and turned to Stefan. He said, "My guys are good to go." Dominicous looked at the others and got the same answer. He focused on Tim. "You can change as you will. They'll send out their shifters, first. I have intel that they don't have many. And we captured the one they valued the most highly. The rest aren't much more than second-rate citizens. They won't fight that hard. In fact, don't be surprised if they take off and hook up with you later. Our faction has overstepped a great many prejudices of late. We are the first in the world to scale these walls. You might have some joiners."

Dominicous glanced at me. "What cover will you provide us?"

"Um." I couldn't help a shrug as I glanced behind me at Toa.

It was Cato who answered from about five feet away. Mage June, his mage, was right beside him. "We will overshadow your advance with spells, of course. I have reason to believe Sasha will lead the assault with me providing the necessary touches to ensure your safety and the enemy's demise, where applicable."

"Are we going in?" I asked Cato.

"We shall see." Cato's eyes crinkled again.

I gave Stefan a put-upon expression and felt our link color with humor and love. I nodded at Dominicous and then Tim before I turned toward Cato. *Showtime*.

"So you guys have been planning this for a while, huh?" I

asked Cato conversationally as the battle commanders broke up and headed to their men.

"Yes. We weren't planning to engage so early, but when you requested aid—well, no time like the present, as they say."

"Who is going in with you?" Paulie asked as he unsheathed his sword. Charles already had his out.

I shook my head and glanced back at the gaggle of magic-workers behind us, most still in the cabbage field. Cato's experienced workers all faced straight ahead, grim and ready. The humans chatted in hushed tones with nervous smiles and shifty eyes, often ogling one of the many warriors standing ready.

"I don't even know that I'm going in. That's what the warriors are for, right?" I turned back to the empty field as Stefan stopped behind Jameson and the giant Kodiac. Ann, the mountain lion, took off at a graceful lope to the right.

"Who's going in?" Paulie repeated.

"Whoever runs that way, bro." Charles looked up and down the line. "Probably just us at first. Birdie will be walking fast toward the fight, you know she will. She'll probably have her hands on her hips and everything. And the twins will go with her, because they rarely know what's going on. They'll just follow. Then some of the others. But they'll be the second tier. Sasha will lead us right into the heart of it."

"We're supposed to stay out here, though, right?" I glanced at Toa before I turned to Cato. "Aren't the magic people supposed to stay back and out of the way?"

"They know you'll see your loved ones charging, and follow." Toa's voice had an edge. "You do not follow protocol at the best of times."

I sighed. I kind of hated that he knew me so well—especially when I was trying to be good.

As the sun climbed, and all the non-humans put on

sunglasses, things went unnaturally still. Thousands of people were gathered, holding swords, staring out at an empty field. A hush fell over the crowd, even the witches and warlocks. Time ground to a halt.

Dominicous glanced back at us.

"It is time." Cato turned his head to me. His faded blue eyes held a ruthless edge. I had never seen the equivalent. I could almost see pain and suffering from hundreds of years past staring out at me. Shivers racked my body. "Trigger the spell. I have up a shield in case the worst happens. Then we will link. *When* we link, you will feel a momentary rush. Your stomach will heave. You will feel disheveled. Maybe dizzy. It is the meeting of two wells of power. It is the connection and fusing of two equal halves. You will see how I do it. You can mimic this with any white, but do so under the best of circumstances if at least one of you isn't experienced."

"I feel like we should've practiced this, because that's not how it is with Toa."

"I am the only person in America that is experienced in this type of link. It is time to learn on the fly, Sasha, as you do so well. Let us begin."

Expectation rode the moment. All of a sudden, this battle took on a completely different feel. It wasn't just about chasing the enemy from our land and rescuing one of ours. This was beyond that—the meeting of two opposite powers. The resuscitation of an old magic that hadn't been used in hundreds of years. The experimentation of Cato's race working with mine. Of making two into one.

I got the distinct impression this was a very beneficial, but very dangerous, superpower.

How do I get myself into these things?

Trying not to focus on possible death a moment away, I turned my attention back to that web of spells created by a master. I sank back into it, just to feel it again. Just to be at one with it for a while longer. And then, with a concentrated effort, I triggered all my dormant spells.

Energy rushed out of me. I felt more bleed in through my link, trying to fill me back up. But more just poured out. Cato reached out to Mage June, steadying himself. The same was most likely happening to him since he'd put his magic into the spells, too.

Nothing happened at first.

The rustle of fabric and people shifting sounded off behind us. A body hit the dirt.

"Take all the energy you can. Release them before you kill them," Cato advised. "You will most likely be cut off when the battle begins, and for that, you should have full energy."

I reached out blindly as I closed my eyes. I felt Charles' hand grab mine before his arm came around my waist to fully support me. I sucked energy from the weaker magic-users first, releasing them when I needed to, as Cato had said. Many fainted, but they'd be fine. Actually, they were probably better off, because once the bloodshed started, they'd most likely freak out. I was helping them.

The air in the field started to shimmer. Like solar flares mixed with heat waves, Cato and my spell was working at the fabric of the spell Nathanial had set. It shimmered and wobbled. Then started to sputter.

I drained off another couple people and started focusing on the larger pools of magic-workers. "Do you have anybody you're not using?" I asked in a pant. "I don't know how long they can hold out."

"Have no fear. We are nearly there."

As if hearing Cato, the draw of energy from the spell started to slow. The pull became less. He'd somehow timed it to take heavily in the beginning, and then taper off. I needed to ask him how when this was all over.

Bursts of light with no sound blazed in ten different spots.

Balloons of white and black swirled through the sky. The draw of energy cut off completely.

Cato straightened up. "Here we go. Nathanial will feel it right—"

CHAPTER EIGHT

"Blast through the wall!"

Jonas braced just inside the door. From the movements, murmurs and scuffles, he guessed probably six people were attempting to find them. One being Nathanial, who Emmy claimed was some expert magic-worker or other. She guessed he would've brought his guards, who were excellent with swords.

Jonas was excellent at killing. He was eager to make their acquaintance.

"Come away from the door," Emmy hissed. "We're leaving out the back."

"The exit is guarded. What's the point?" Jonas whispered back. The timbre of his voice, though, carried.

The shuffling beyond the walls silenced. Then, "Emmy, my darling. You have greatly vexed me. It would be wise if you left your barbarian and returned to me. I'll go easy on you, my dear."

Jonas shifted impatiently. He wanted to rip that smug voice out of that male's throat.

"You disappoint me, Emilia." A spark of light seeped

through the door before a small blast echoed through the tunnels. The dull sounds of stone falling rumbled across the floor. Dust shifted down from the ceiling and settled like ash across Jonas' shoulders. A few pebbles followed, along with a deep, low groan of rock shifting.

"You'll bring this whole place down on top of us!" Emmy yelled.

Jonas could see her in the dim glow of light shifting under the door. She frantically waved Jonas back toward a square patch of deeper black. If they went through that door, they would then just trap themselves between the guards at the exit, and the mage tracking her with magic. There would be more to take on, and the result would probably be the same.

He motioned her through. Time had run out. "You go. I'll see what damage I can do."

He could just see the plane of Emmy's face shift toward him, following the sound of his voice. She couldn't see any better than before, even with the swaying and bouncing light from under the door. But he could. He could see her straighten up in resignation. Straighten her shoulders and lift her head. He saw her step forward and untie the whips from around her waist.

He could see her get ready for battle. She wouldn't leave him. She'd fight her greatest fear, right beside him.

What a fucking great female. Also, a stupid one. "Run!" he seethed. "It isn't worth your life."

"There is nowhere *to* run. Not from me." That smug voice floated in the darkness. A foot interrupted the light beneath the door.

Jonas let magic pulse through him. His arms swirled in orange. His hands formed claws in front of him. Someone was about to get a facelift.

A hand hit the door. It swung open with the customary squeal. Jonas jumped forward as the earth rumbled. Then shook. A loud explosion thundered through the walls and rolled through the air. Jonas grabbed a male's face and took a cheek with him as he was flung against a wall. The low tremor was interrupted with screaming.

The ceiling above them groaned. Small rocks rained down in warning. Dust sifted through the air. Somewhere, stone crumbled and littered across the floor. The earth rumbled again. The ceiling groaned louder in absolute misery. Jonas was flung to the other side of the room.

Sasha had arrived.

"We're being attacked!" Nathanial screamed. He wasn't so smug now. "Forget the girl. Get to your battle positions."

"This whole place is going to come down." Emmy dashed toward the open door on nimble feet as the world stilled for a moment.

"No!" Jonas reached for her and missed. He stood to chase only to stop dead as she ducked and snatched up a sword much too big for her body. She held it out to him.

"C'mon, hurry!" After he grabbed the sword, she dashed past him to the small open door at the back of the room. "They'll leave that exit to get their battle gear. We need to get through before this place comes down on our heads!"

With a quick glance at the now-swordless male holding his bloody cheek and writhing on the ground, Jonas took after an extremely resourceful female. They ran at full speed through twists and turns she seemed to know by heart.

"He just abandoned you when he was right on top of you?" Jonas asked as he struggled to keep up. She had shorter legs, was a female, and had inherited mostly human strength, but damned if she wasn't faster than he was.

"His magic is invested in the defense of this place. If someone starts messing with the spells, it's going to mess with his magic. If they hit him just right—and hopefully they did—it's going to drain his power. Or whatever. He has to link so he doesn't go down with the ship. With all the explosions, if your mage even half knows what she's doing, he won't have a lot of time."

"She doesn't. But she's with people who do."

Emmy slowed to a walk as a large patch of daylight crept up the hall. Up ahead about fifty feet was a huge hole in the wall that might've once been a doorway. Three dead guards lay strewn around the opening, two having been crushed under pieces of the wall, and one with a stone lodged in half his face. They probably hadn't seen it coming.

"Holy shit," Emmy breathed, starting to jog again. "*Someone* sure knows what they're about."

Jonas couldn't help a swelling of pride. Sasha made shit up on the fly, but when she got into making a point, she really went all out. This spoke of her like nothing else would.

With freedom waiting beyond the opening, and a groaning collection of walls and ceiling behind them, Emmy put on a burst of speed into the bright sunlight. Laughing with glee, she put up her hands and reached for the sky. A second later, she gave a terrified scream and put her hands up to shield her face.

"No!" Jonas yelled in horror.

I stared in wonder at a large, three-story building with gaping holes dotting the front. The dust hadn't even settled before people were staggering out like drunk ants, waving swords, squinting, and shaking their heads. They probably should've taken a second to recover, though, because our guys were already running at a full sprint to any opening they saw.

"Okay, Sasha, let's link." Cato turned to me and put out his hand like a handshake. "It is easier if we have physical contact the first few times."

I saw Stefan and Dominicous start jogging forward with the last line of their warriors, swords drawn, tattoos blazing. My heart leapt in my throat. My muscles started to tingle. I had to go. I had to go with them. I couldn't let them go in alone.

"Link, Sasha," the calm but insistent voice implored.

"Are you sure this is a good idea, sir?" Mage June asked.

Paulie shifted where he stood. His knuckles were white around the handle of his sword. Charles stared at me, not moving, not showing his impatience, waiting for my cue. He was the more experienced of the two. He knew what was important, what needed to happen before the charge, and he was staring at me with expectancy.

I turned my face toward Cato with barely-contained impatience. With those faded-blue eyes, shining with a terrible light of death and destruction, backed with knowledge and wisdom, he was more prepared for battle than any person on this battle field. I could see past bloodshed haunting his vision. I could almost *feel* the deadly spells churning in his memory.

I reached out and took his old, wrinkled hand. His magic reached for mine. And he'd been right—it wasn't like when I linked with Toa. For one, the link delved deeper until it clutched at my root. It seemed to wrap around the base of me in a firm grip. At the same time, his magic implored that I reach forward and do the same to him. Equal. Balanced.

I followed his lead, so easy when I could see it being done. No lectures, just *doing*.

"Strong connection. Good work." Cato closed his eyes.

Toa stepped forward to brace his shoulders while throwing Charles a *look*. That's when it happened. My world heaved. My stomach roiled and my head swam. I felt like I was floating and sinking at the same time. Like I couldn't get enough breath. Focusing on Charles' hands on my shoulders,

I squeezed my eyes shut and gave in to it. I felt the foreign type of magic seep into and wrap around mine. It was almost like the two forms of magic were threading their fingers together.

Within a few seconds, the feeling cleared. I opened my eyes to a smiling, though still serious, Cato. "Excellent. That went off marvelously. And just in time. It seems our number one enemy has advanced."

Cato turned and started walking, slowly, toward the battlefield. Fighting raged before us. Flashes of magic and swinging swords were often followed by splashes of deep crimson flying through the bright sky. Within the casing of a window on the second floor of the building, which was about fifty yards from the street, stood one man in a bright white robe. Equally-bright white magic rolled and boiled between his hands before a floating orb descended toward the battlefield. Toward Jameson, who fought directly below on the dais, working his way into the building!

Without thinking, just reacting, I rocketed out a mix of water and earth to smother that ball while I quickly unraveled it. But it wasn't just me. I felt the deft touch of Cato, not following on my coattails this time, but working *with* me. Right beside me. As if we had the same magical body and four hands with which to work the spells.

My smothering wrapped around the orb with a black sheen as a white gloss worked within. I could feel Cato tweaking and manipulating my spell with that complex mastery that he was known for. Within seconds, the orb fizzled into nothing. Jameson, none the wiser, slashed through the neck of a woman in front of him and charged into the building.

The man in the white robe looked around wildly. His robes were disturbed in the wind.

"Surprise, you bastard!" I started throwing out spells

without a second thought—hitting those on the battlefield standing in the way of our guys. Cato was always there, working with me. Improving me. Helping me learn.

"Nathanial is drawing off of a group of... I would say four powerful mages." Cato's eyes went distant. He was working on my spells while figuring out the enemy.

If I didn't think I was a novice before, this would be a rude awakening.

"None of them have the power like we do, or he wouldn't be struggling with the flux. He works. That is helpful."

"So... can we attack him, or what? I can blow up the ledge he's standing on pretty easily."

Paulie's fast movement caught my eye. He ripped something out of his belt and pointed it straight ahead. A moment later the loud *boom* of a gun blasted across the battlefield. More than one person flinched. The man that was running at Dominicous' back, sword drawn, jerked back as a blossom of blood appeared in the center of his chest.

Charles looked at Paulie with wide eyes. "You brought a gun?"

Paulie shrugged, watching the battle with fervent eyes. "It doesn't do much on magic, sure, but it sure cuts through the bullshit with flesh and blood."

"Hide it again, son," Cato said with strain in his voice. "Magic can be used to render such objects useless. At least hard to handle. Use it sparingly and only against those who are not as fluent in magic."

Paulie slipped the weapon back into his belt.

"Now. The fun begins." Cato blast off a spell to a man I hadn't noticed in a third floor window containing no glass. It wrapped around him with stinging fire, but not as potent as I would've liked. I added my crude violence to the spell to finish it up.

The man screamed and clawed at his body. Nathanial staggered and looked in the direction of his counterpart even though he wouldn't have been able to see from his vantage point. A moment later, his head slowly tilted down to our location. And then sighted Cato. A grim smile lit up the handsome face.

Game on.

A spell whipped off toward us so fast I couldn't even think. I couldn't react. I stood there stupidly as white and black swirling magic interceded and tore it apart before it could reach us.

"You see, each of us can work with our combined might. We do not have to be next to each other to use our combined magic," Cato replied calmly as two spells I didn't recognize zipped back toward that ledge. They never reached the man.

Another intricate spell came firing back at us. "We're a standing target!" I jumped from foot to foot. I wanted to throw a rock. At least he couldn't disintegrate a rock!

Could he?

"He is also standing still. This is a magical duel and his ingenuity has grown. Sadly, mine has not. I can barely keep his attacks off of us. It is time for you to earn your reputation, Sasha. Find a way to cut him down."

My mouth dropped open as a beautiful layer of mist sped our way. I threw up a shield at the last minute but Cato had already disbanded it. The shield wouldn't have worked, anyway. That spell had magical drills. He was expecting a shield, and it would've bored right through mine.

Shit. He was so far above me I was in awe. How the hell was I supposed to stop him?

"C'mon, Sasha!" Charles grabbed my arm and ripped me forward. "You're in your head. Nothing good comes when you think. Let's get moving. Get the blood flowing. I need to kill something."

"Amen," Paulie said, jogging with us.

Charles was right. I didn't stand still and wait for spells to come to me. I... did other things. Like run around like an idiot. Things always seemed to work out that way. Somehow.

"Okay. Nathanial is kicking our ass magic-wise. So a sword in his back is warranted, I think. Also, we need to get Jonas out of there. So... into the belly!" I took out my sword and applied a burst of speed. We had a thick crowd of aggressive enemy to get through before we even made it to the building. It'd take a second.

I zipped off blasts of fire to stun two huge guys in front of me before firing off a nasty, spiky spell toward Mr. Wizard and his stupid white robe. As Charles and Paulie stepped forward to stab the men, I watched Nathanial stagger on his perch as his shield was hit and *raked* by my spell. Before he could turn his head in the direction of the spell, Cato had used the distraction to fire a spell of his own.

"We have to keep moving. That Nathanial can throw spells without looking, I'd bet. And I won't be able to—" A snowflake-looking spell flew toward me. I didn't know what it was, what it did, or how to get rid of it.

"Run!" I screamed. I pushed the boys into a wall of men and then blasted my way through. Limbs went everywhere— thank God they were all once attached to the enemy at one time and not my guys. Plants sprang up out of the ground and started to grow into the monsters they'd become. Fireworks and distracting spells crackled in the sky. An explosion blasted the building right next to Nathanial.

Yes, I had done all of that. No, I did not remember initiating any of those spells. Death was on my doorstep, and he wore an absurd white robe.

CHAPTER NINE

All else forgotten, Jonas launched through the door. His bare chest met a furry body. They both hit the ground and rolled. Jonas was up first, standing in front of Emmy with his hands out wide and his eyes on fire. The wolf he'd tackled rolled to its feet as another two stared at him with hackles raised and teeth bared.

"You Tim's lot?" Jonas asked in a growl. "Because if so, I won't kill you."

The wolf closest, which still had dirt in its coat, huffed. It shook out its body. The growls from the other two cut off.

"Right. Emmy is on our side. Carry on." Jonas glanced back at Emmy. Her face was pale but her mouth was set in grim determination.

She unslung her whips. "Rookie mistake," she muttered.

"Time to get bloody, baby. Ready?" Jonas connected gazes with her. Something in his chest shifted—he felt grounded. And with her at his back, though she'd probably never really fought a day in her life, he felt guarded. She had his back. He had hers.

He couldn't help a smile.

She grinned back. "You're crazy."

"Yup. Let's go. Mongrels—there's nothing in that way. It's the dungeon and a maze. Get me to Sasha."

The lead wolf growled once—its version of talking back—before it turned to the north and started loping at a fast pace. Jonas grabbed his sword off the ground and wasted no time, not bothering to look behind him to make sure Emmy was keeping up. And in another few seconds, he didn't have to look back at all—he was the last in line. Damn, but the female was fast.

They took a turn around a corner as the noise of battle increased. Sword clanks and explosions drifted from the distant front of the building—they must've exited in the back. Other than a couple dead warriors with ripped-out throats no one lingered on this side. As they neared the middle of the building, though, Jonas could see fighting through the holes in the side of the structure. His guys had found their way in already! It was looking good.

That thought abruptly shifted as they came to the next corner and saw the larger battle in progress. Vicious, grisly fighting covered the front of the building. Blood pooled and ran in rivulets along the packed dirt. Magic soared and exploded overhead, white and black. Attack spells of all kinds zinged through the fighting, taking out warriors in nasty ways.

Jonas spotted a huge bear rending through a line to get into the building. He saw Cato a ways off, in the street surrounded by magic-workers, all working with fast hand movements as they looked up.

Jonas followed their gaze to a man in a white robe with a grim but expectant expression.

"That's Nathanial," Emmy said at his side. She was looking where he was. "He's better than them. I'd feared he was. They won't be able to take him with magic."

Jonas swept the road with his gaze for Sasha or Charles. His stomach started to knot when he didn't find her with the other magic-workers. Hesitantly, knowing what he would see, he then looked harder at the battle. As he did so, he saw a flash of green unfurl right before a dull roar. A plant grew upwards into the sky, drawing shocked glances.

"She's in the thick of it. *Shit!* She's probably trying to go after that magic-worker." Jonas glanced up at the robed worker before looking back to the fighting crowd. He glanced ahead of the plant and saw the door she must be trying to reach. She probably only had Charles with her, and possibly Paulie.

"She is such an idiot." Adrenaline filled Jonas' body. He flexed and tightened his grip on his sword. He then turned slowly to Emmy.

Her beautiful blue eyes were pools of worry and fear. Her face was even whiter than before as she glanced up at Nathanial and then back at the bloody spectacle before the building. She was way out of her league.

"Go hide," Jonas said softly. "Stay safe. You're free now. When this is over, no matter what happens, find someone loyal to Cato and say you need Nathanial's tracker off of you. I have plenty of money and everything you could possibly need. Find someone from—"

Emmy slapped him across the face. Red blotches appeared on her cheeks. "Don't be daft. I'm going to kill that sonuvabitch Nathanial and *earn* my place among your people. Lead the way to this Sasha."

"You don't know how to—" Another slap cut Jonas off. "Fair enough."

With a grin he couldn't suppress, he glanced down at the wolves. "You guys going or what?"

With a huff, they took off running. Jonas followed immediately, sword out. In ten paces he reached his first opponent.

A sword slashed out, fast and controlled. These guys were an experienced and adjusted class of warrior, if this male was any judge. Of good stock, too. But very... cultivated. Boring.

Jonas knocked the sword to the side and rushed forward with glowing arms. Adrenaline and Emmy's essence pumped within him. Made him feel stronger and faster. Better. He gored his fingers through the eyes and then ripped down the face. He brought his sword around and stuck it in the male's gut before he was moving on. He stuck the next warrior, a large female with lightning fast movements and then retreated a step when someone else rushed him. A crack rent the air. A red and white stream of blood and fluid gushed out of the male's eye socket. Another crack, immediately after the first, took out the other eye.

Jonas couldn't help a half-second to gawk.

Emmy ran right by him. He was surrounded by survivors in this life, it seemed. And they made the best warriors.

The two of them and the three wolves cut through the front of the building. Aiming for the line that would intersect with the whirling and sizzling cacophony of magic. Nathanial was throwing things down at Sasha and she was answering as only she could—completely unpredictably.

"She's way out of her league," Emmy yelled. "Is that a *dinosaur?*"

"She's new to all this and she doesn't have any real teachers. Yeah, she's way out of her league. But she'll rally."

"Not for long." Emmy pointed to the road. Cato staggered and went down on one knee. She then pointed directly overhead at Nathanial. He turned slowly. Too slowly, it seemed like. White was building around him. His focus shifted to the cluster of warriors and the one mage, struggling to fight her way through. Jonas saw the pale gold of Charles' sword, and the gold of another sword—Paulie.

"No!" Jonas yelled. He looked at the building, trying to

find a ledge or something to climb up on. Gauging the distance between him and the white mage. It was too far to throw a sword. He turned to Emmy. "Can you throw a knife?"

Emmy took out a knife and jogged to the side, out from under the overhang. A male rushed toward her. A furry gray body interceded, taking the man down, but another was there. Jonas lunged but Emmy had already turned and stuck her knife in his throat.

The spell was a white arrow, created and waiting on the order to send. Nathanial leaned forward with bent arms. Here came the push.

The strangled yell got caught in Jonas' throat as the spell burst forward. A loud *boom* sounded, like a gunshot. Nathanial staggered back as red blossomed on his shoulder—Paulie had shot him. The spell was already let loose, though.

"C'mon!" Jonas screamed. He grabbed Emmy and yanked her with him. He stabbed and clawed his way through enemy as if they were *papier-mâché*. Emmy rallied right behind him, clearing out the cluster with precise whip-strikes to vital areas. Still that spell fell.

The cluster of people around Sasha broke up. Warriors staggered and crawled out of the way. Running from that spell. A hole was left in the middle where three people stood. One small human, and her two large bodyguards, staring at that spell descending straight for them.

"Sasha!" Jonas recognized the Boss' hoarse scream. It was distant, though. The Boss couldn't help this time. No one could.

I stared at that arrow of death. The spell whirled and twirled. Nathanial had taken his time with this one. Concocted an exquisite torture device that would melt off my skin and boil my bones. Very pleasant.

Time slowed down. I heard Jonas scream for me from somewhere, and then Stefan. *Good, they're still alive.*

My gaze rose to the man on the ledge. Red squeezed up through his fingers as he held his shoulder. A condescending smile was aimed down at me.

Rage boiled up. And then cleared. I remembered the feel of his magic from the spell around the building. I recalled how he constructed his traps. His viciousness and showmanship.

Showmanship.

He was intricate, but did that help anything? Or was it just lipstick and mascara?

I *felt* that spell hurtling toward me. I thought about the components and what he was trying to do. I remembered the way Cato dressed up my crude spells and added flourishes and embellishments. Mine and Cato's had only necessary elements.

Half the crap in that arrow wasn't necessary. It was showmanship. It was stroking a huge ego.

Sweat beaded my brow as that thing thundered down toward me. I had five heartbeats.

I closed my eyes and forced Cato and my magic into that spell. I rooted around. I felt things. I played. I toyed. I just *felt*.

Like a flash of light in the darkness, it suddenly made sense. His thinking, his way of bending magic, his flourish—it made sense. And it still had the crude base, it was just covered with the sleight of hand and trickery of a Las Vegas show.

I'd never be able to disentangle, but I could alter. I could change a few major components in the hardwiring to render it into a completely different kind of spell.

I ripped and gouged with my now-balanced magic. I knocked the spell off-kilter and then stuffed in changes. I soaked the thing in the perfect yin and yang of Cato and my link. And then I held my breath.

The arrow fell onto me like a puff of dragon breath. It billowed out and around Charles, Paulie and I, and then detonated. Instead of an acid pour, the air around us erupted in sparkles. Pinks and blues and purples, it was like a rave and glitter party rolled into one.

"What the hell? I look like a chick!" Charles stared down at his shimmery hands.

"At least you're not dead. Send him back something terrible, Sasha, and let's get under cover." Paulie glanced down at his gun, which had started to smoke and sputter. It was only a matter of time before the heat spell reacted with the gunpowder in the bullets. But the shot had been worth it.

I rolled a collection of Toa's delights into a tight ball, with my special touch, and sent it off. Nathanial would unravel it, since I didn't have that protective flourish around it, but it would take him a minute. I glanced back at Cato, who was staring out at me. He gave me one nod. Then he shifted his focus back to Nathanial.

He'd seen what I did, and he'd probably be pretty sparkly himself soon.

I started running toward the door. "Let's get to that asshole and take him out with something sharp!"

CHAPTER TEN

Jonas saw Sasha sprinting toward the building with a mostly clear line. No one had recovered as quickly as she had—the original spell must've been a real nasty one. The enemy seemed to know what to expect. But it hadn't landed.

With a grin, Jonas started sprinting to meet her. Emmy kept right at his side, wielding her whip better than most people would use a sword or pencil. She slashed and cut people ten feet away and had them flinching to the sides as she, Jonas and three wolves ran through.

Ten feet now. He could see Sasha's dirty and determined face. Charles, blood-spattered and gritty, stabbed a large male guarding one of the entrances. And then Jonas was upon them. He stabbed a female in the back, ripped her out of the way, and burst into the space of Paulie. The halfsie spun and thrust a sword toward Jonas' gut.

"It's me, human!" Jonas growled as he knocked the strike aside. "Damn you're slow."

A relieved twinkle lighted Paulie's eyes as Sasha exclaimed, "Oh thank God, Jonas!"

She launched her small body into his arms with a fierce

hug. Jonas squeezed her back, filled with a sense of joy and relief he couldn't remember the equal.

"Glad to have ya back, bro, but we gotta go. That white mage is no joke." Charles stepped forward and slapped Jonas on the back.

A whip cracked to their right, drawing all of their focus to Emmy. Using both hands equally well, she slashed and flayed anyone running within her circle of violence. Two males waited just outside her reach, watching her with wary eyes, preparing to charge. They knew her capabilities.

Sasha backed off of Jonas long enough to squint at Emmy. Jonas' stomach did a strange flip-flop of uncertainty before Sasha said, "Ah. The tracker. I see it now. What a sneaky devil."

"Can you take it off?" Jonas asked in a gruff voice.

Charles started laughing as he rushed forward to charge the men eyeing Emmy. He dispatched one as Emmy stepped forward and snapped the eye out of the other. Over the screaming, Charles said, "Worried about the human not liking your lady-love, huh, bro?"

"You analyzing feelings like a chick, now?" Jonas growled.

"Tracker's gone. That was an easy one. He didn't put all his stupid swirly hogwash on it. Speaking of, let's go kill him." Sasha slapped Jonas on the back, winked at Emmy in welcome, and then motioned everyone forward.

We entered the building at a half-jog. As we emerged into the low light and shadow, I lost visibility as my eyes struggled to adjust. I ducked off to the side and stepped into an empty room. The others followed me and waited for the wolves to get through before shutting and locking the door.

"Okay. Regroup." I caught my breath and willed my eyes

to adjust faster. After being in the sunlight I absolutely hated this terrible low light. "We have Jonas, so we'll call that mission accomplished."

Charles nodded. Jonas had found us, but we'd still take the "W" on that one.

"Now. We need to get up to the second floor and get that creep. Without him we can clean this place up." I turned my gaze to the stupidly beautiful woman huddled next to Jonas. A freaking knock-out was this girl, but sad-looking. Kind of hunched and broken. Her eyes were shadowed and haunted and she didn't seem to feel comfortable with Charles standing next to her. It was almost as if she tried to physically lower herself to make him look more powerful.

And judging by his preening, Charles was feeling masterful and had no idea why.

I rolled my eyes. "Charles, you're making—Emmy? You're making Emmy nervous. Get away."

"Why? What did I do?" Charles gave her a wounded look as he moved to my other side.

"Emmy, can you get us there?" I asked in what I hoped was a soft voice.

"If you treat her like a victim, she'll feel like a victim. If you treat her like a vigilante, she'll get her revenge and move on." Paulie stood near the door, listening for what was happening on the other side.

Jonas threw him an approving glance.

"Oh, well, excuse me for trying to be sensitive." I rubbed my forehead.

"As sensitive as a steel mace," Charles muttered.

Emmy's expression went from shy vulnerability to blatant confusion.

"There is nothing that is professional with this gang." Paulie grinned at Emmy. "Get used to it. And now the humans have the dominance."

"Not at all, bro." Charles adjusted his sword in his sheath. "We got two of the awesome race plus two additional halves of the awesome race, versus one whole and two halves of the virus race. Three to two."

"Virus race?" I glowered at Charles. "Really? And congratulations on being able to do math. I suppose you'll have to go take a nap now to recuperate."

"I will admit that the one whole human is way bitchier than everyone else put together. Trials of the species."

"I'll show you bitchy." Willing calm, I turned back to Emmy. Disbelief had replaced the confusion. "Can you get us there?"

"Yes," she said softly.

"Then let's do this. We're wasting time." Jonas glanced at Paulie. "You're shit with that sword. What else you got?"

"Just my winning personality."

"Magic?"

"I'm linked with Sasha to give her energy, so she holds the magical focus."

Jonas glanced at Emmy's knives and then her whips. "Then work with Emmy. She'll stun people while you poke them. Otherwise, you won't last much longer, human."

"Why do you call everyone human?" Emmy asked quietly.

Jonas face melted into one of concern as he looked down on her.

"Because he is a rotten ol' bastard without a nice bone in his body. Get used to it," I said as I moved to the door. "If he starts using my name, I won't know who he is. Okay, we need to end this fight. Enough stalling."

"I am not in a hurry to face that mage again, though." Charles stepped in closer.

"Me either, but we have to. No one should be allowed to be that good."

Paulie opened the door a crack and then closed it immediately. He took a deep breath and moved away from the door. Jonas took his place in a swirl of orange power. Everyone braced.

Jonas ripped the door open and burst out. Charles went next followed by me, magic spell to kill at the ready. Charles stabbed someone in the back as Jonas ripped someone else off the ground and threw him. I burst through with a spell and ran smack into Stefan, Jameson, and the huge bear that was Tim. They knew we were in there and were coming for us.

I probably should've felt that, but I was just a bit off my game...

When Stefan saw me emerge, he ripped me toward him and crushed me to his chest. "I thought he had you. Jesus, Sasha, I thought he had you."

I gave myself five full seconds of his tight embrace, feeling his warmth and safety hugged around me. Feeling our hearts beating rapidly together. Then I pushed away and composed myself. "Oh ye of little faith."

His dark eyes stared down at me, touching the deep part of me no one else could get to. A fog of desire enveloped me.

"Not the time, human," Jonas growled.

"Right." I sighed and tore my eyes away from my love. Battle still raged around us, kept away for the moment by Tim's crew of snarling, ravaging shifters.

I looked back up at Stefan. "I gotta go."

"I know. We're going with you. We're dominating in battle, but losing in magic. Cato is on his knees. We don't have much time."

A shock of guilt and adrenaline both pierced me. I turned back to Emmy, who had melted against the door. She really didn't seem to like the presence of Stefan's race, especially those in the leadership role.

Time to get over that ridiculousness. "Okay, Emmy, you're

up. And don't worry about, like, social stuff. Okay? We're all equals, here."

"Hardly." Charles lifted his eyebrows when he saw mine and Jonas' glare. "We pride those with more talent over those without. That's all I meant!"

Jonas held out his hand. Emmy grasped it, immediately. Jameson and Stefan's eyes both went completely round. I snickered. Jonas had found *lurve*. How cute.

Charles and I would totally bust his balls!

In the next moment, as Emmy began to move with purpose, my smile melted back into my mask of determination. With the shifters shadowing her sides, and rushing ahead to clear a path, and the rest of us directly behind, we all moved as a unit through a wide hallway to the middle of the building.

"We can trust her, right, bro?" Charles muttered in a low tone.

If Jonas answered, I couldn't hear. Screaming drowned out my thoughts as we passed an intersecting corridor in view of a wide set of stairs. A mage had some of our guys on the ground, blasting them with a spell that caused convulsions and the blistering of skin. The mage in question was completely calm as he tortured those on the floor at his feet.

My stomach turned as I whipped out a circular array of electric current. As the spell was released, the mage turned toward us to hurl something. He never got the chance. A crack had a sickening line of red opening on his throat. The skin seemed to blister as it turned away from the whip slash. He gurgled out a scream and clutched at his throat as my spell hit, electrocuting him on the spot and stopping all his vitals.

"You learned some nasty spells, human," Jonas said as we pushed forward.

"There are a lot of them here. I've made mine at least kill quickly."

"The group elected to come to this compound are the best. The best at fighting, and the best at offensive spells." Emmy took the stairs two at a time. "They intended to take the Council. I don't think they expected the Council to come to them. They usually underestimate Americans. Always have."

"Well, good for us," I said.

We found an empty hallway at the top of the stairs, which immediately had me grabbing Emmy by the back of the gown (odd choice of clothes) to slow her. I veered to the side. Stefan and Jameson stepped in front of us. Jonas walked lightly to the other side. The shifters, one and all, put their noses to the ground.

"Nathanial is too good to leave his back unguarded," I whispered as my magic drifted down the hall in front of us. "Which way is it?"

"Straight down the hall to the middle, left through a door, down a hall, and then up a few steps and over to the ledge."

"Do you know who guards him in battle?" Stefan asked softly.

"The man you just killed is one. He probably descended from the top of the stairs. Then Nathanial will have five with swords, and I don't know how many magical people."

"Cato said four, but we took two down," I said.

Emmy shook her head. "He has replacements always ready. He can only hold a certain power level in a link, so when someone falters, he brings on someone else in their place.

"Do you have a blood bond?" Stefan looked at her keenly. "Will he know you're coming?"

Emmy shook her head again, a look of pure disgust crossing her face. "If the black mage took off the tracker, then no. I have never taken his blood—he has only taken mine."

Stefan nodded and glanced at Jonas. We were all wondering if Emmy could be trusted. Being *kept* was a funny thing—you might hate your captor, but if that was all you knew, change could be scary. And fear made a person do irrational things. I trusted Jonas, but Emmy was very pretty, and very good with Jonas' sexual pleasure of choice. It would be easy for his male anatomy to make decisions his brain never would.

We didn't have much choice, though. The best course of action now was to keep her close. Keep her where we could see her.

Stefan glanced at me, wariness bleeding through the link. I nodded slightly, letting him know I followed his thinking, before we took off again. Toward the middle of the corridor my magic fizzled and sparked. I pulled it back enough to lighten my perception—using heavy magic could be like stepping on a land mine for some traps. If you hit it and then pulled it away, the bomb went boom. Thankfully, Toa made me learn this the hard way. And the lesson had hurt. A lot.

I walked forward softly. Everyone else shadowed, trusting my lead. Toward the middle of the corridor, I once again *felt*. It was the only way I could decipher this lunatic's spells. The normal twirly-swirly was there, making unraveling extremely time-consuming. The crude foundation was, indeed, an explosion. Also, a marker. When it went *boom*, it would alert the owner that someone was coming.

I let my balanced magic seep into his spell, changing certain characteristics, while extending my feelers beyond the door. Another trap waited. Luckily, the same one.

"Tim, can you smell anyone beyond the door? Bears are supposed to have one of the best olfactory systems, right?" I whispered as sweat beaded my brow. I cut my link from a couple more people. Energy was starting to be a factor.

Tim gave a deep huff as his large, shaggy body stepped even with me. He sniffed next to the wall, higher, and then to the ground. He swung his head from side to side.

"No, you can't get a reading at all, or no, no one is there?"

He stared at me. This was the problem with shifters—communication outside of their crew was kind of a pain.

"Okay, so, two shakes for the first, one shake for the second..." I helped.

I got one shake. Fine.

Another minute had the spells giving a wonderful light show, and then springing into a tiny plant monster. "Why do I always make plant monsters?"

Charles stepped forward and slashed it to pieces. "Because of the inverted magic, remember?"

"But plant monsters? Why not a Carebear or something else?" I opened the door and quickly moved aside so Charles could take out mini-plant-monster number two.

"You are extraordinarily advanced for being able to work with Nathanial's magic. But yet, you seem so naïve..." Emmy ducked through the corridor at Jonas' beckoning.

"You can say it. I don't know what I'm doing. Go ahead. I'm not offended." I scowled as I followed the others, spreading out my magic in front of me. *Everybody's a critic.*

"You should've been around when she was first learning," Charles whispered with a smile.

I punched him. And it made me feel better that he grunted and rubbed his side.

"The nature of their fighting relationship takes some getting used to," Jameson said in a soft voice.

Tim huffed.

We continued down the hall in near-silence. In fact, I got constant looks because I was the loudest one. Even Paulie had the absolute stealth down. Emmy, too. And how a giant bear, who nearly took up the corridor on his own, could be silent I had no idea. But none of this was making me look good.

"The final door is up here at the top of the stairs. It will open up into a large square room. He'll have all his linked mages with him, probably." Emmy chewed her lip. "I don't know about the guards. I would assume some would be with him, but some should be guarding the door…"

Another trap lay in wait, this one much more advanced than the others. Still the same construction, though. These were all laid by Nathanial. "He doesn't like delegating, huh?"

"He links and always works the majority of the important spells. He doesn't trust others to do it."

I could barely hear her whisper. Her body was starting to shake and her hands gripped her whips tightly. Worse, Jonas was getting very edgy. His thick cords of muscles were flexed up and down his body and his arms had come away from his sides. Signs that he was about to lose his shit. Charles took a step away.

"You know a lot about him," Jameson said lightly. I wasn't fooled. He sensed a trap.

Stefan blasted wariness and uncertainty through our link.

"I was kept as his prisoner. I know a great deal," she said in a hush, trembling all over.

And she was treated abominably, I'd bet. My heart went out to the girl. Facing a tormentor took the greatest of courage. I hoped she had it, and didn't, instead, cower and give us away. I didn't want Jonas to have to lose the one woman he'd let himself love. Because there would never be another. Not for him. He wasn't the type of guy to move on from deep anguish and torment. He owned his misery like a cloak, constantly overcoming it when it threatened to take him over. He didn't move on all that easily.

Clearing my mind, because there was nothing I could do, I worked at that spell as I crept forward. I put my hand on Tim's shoulder and moved him up with me. When I stopped, he did likewise. "Can you smell anyone?"

His big head nodded yes. And then he bristled.

"One nod per different smell," Stefan murmured.

Ten nods. We had more people, but less magic workers. I knew it.

"I wonder if Cato is still active." I focused on our link and tried to trace it to him. It was a partnership, so that didn't work. But I did know he was alive. And that's all I knew.

"The man in the white cloak was taking out our guys while dueling Cato," Jameson said softly. "If it was a full attack on only Cato, he would be long since dead. As it is, he probably isn't far away."

"That mage is shot, though. That'll slow him down," Paulie said.

A normal man, yes, but not this guy. I had every belief he'd rule pain like he ruled his people—not much would slow that mage down. He didn't get as good as he was without constant diligence and complete focus on the matter at hand.

Urgency squeezed my chest as the last trap turned into a puddle of magic and drifted away. "Hmm. That was the best yet. I'm learning."

The door burst open. Three men poured out with swords drawn.

Spoke too soon!

Stefan pushed me to the side and took my place at the top. But we had a bear. A really big, angry, alpha bear.

Tim lumbered forward with a roar that shook the walls. I heard a yell from the battlefield below. Our guys knew what that sound meant.

Tim stood, taking up most of the corridor from side-to-side and top-to-bottom. He swung his massive paw and swiped the face off of the first guy. Jonas jetted under another huge swipe and stabbed an enemy in the gut as Tim took the guts out of someone else then pushed forward, stepping on squirming bodies and getting a chop in the neck from a man trying to get out to the fray. The huge bear roared again with anger and determination.

I blasted the whole wall, knocking rubble into the room and a hole in the ceiling. Tiles and plaster rained down on us as our guys forced their way into the room behind and to the sides of Tim. I was crowded with Emmy between Charles, Jonas and Paulie as the three pushed us in after the others.

The room opened up like Emmy had said. One figure stood at the ledge on the far side. Crimson leaked down his arm and the tail-end of a really nasty spell left the circling of his arms. A sword came at my head as the robed man turned around slowly.

At that moment the world went dizzy. My stomach heaved. And then the perfect balance, the harmony of magic, eroded away. I was left without the other half. With just my own.

Someone fell dead at my feet, but I didn't even notice. A sob ripped out of my throat as I met the cold, calculating eyes of the man who'd just killed Cato. Nathanial now had all his attention on me.

CHAPTER ELEVEN

"No!" I screamed.

"A human. To challenge me? Why-o-why did they bother to let you out of your cage?" His smile became placating. "What will you do without your puppet-master, little puppet?"

Faster than thought, a blast of white came at me. I plunged into it with my opposite magic and imploded the damn thing. I knew what he was about. I might be a human hack, but I was a destructive one.

"Puppet-master? That is so cliché," I said with a sneer as I took a step forward and blended two of Toa's really, *really* nasty spells. I added my own flourish—a bunch of jumbled, magical crap all heaped on top with little zings and blasts of magic. No pretty wrapping that he'd be used to, no. A bunch of spare parts and forgotten bits that would affront this sensibilities. *So suck it!*

Tim roared and attacked one of the mages huddling against the wall. "Let me disengage!" the man screamed as the bear descended.

Stefan dodged a swinging sword, stepped over a wolf, and

plunged his sword into an enemy's gut as Jonas launched himself at another mage running toward the door.

"But I need your magic," Nathanial sneered as his face clouded with my spell. "How ab-solutely *revolting* is this spell?"

"I hate how you all drag out the word absolutely. It drives me nuts." Another spell came at me as mine fell away. And then Nathanial glanced at Tim and flicked his wrist.

"Did you know, stupid human, that the mastery of magic can force a shifter into his own body? A lesser species, to be sure." Another spell came at me and exploded halfway to me as Tim erupted in a cloud of green. In the place of the bear lay a naked and shocked human.

Nathanial laughed as I wrestled with the next spell. Even just blowing things up or changing them, he was too good. Too experienced. Too fast. I was flying by the seat of my pants, and he knew it. He devised his spells accordingly. He aimed to take time. To make me think. He was the best mage in the world against, arguably, the most new and naïve. I didn't stand a chance.

Spells zipped off toward Stefan and Jameson as the rest of the shifters were forced to change into their human, expending massive amounts of energy to do so. The shock of blue hair in the corner meant Ann was alive, but not much use.

"Paulie, do you have your gun?" I asked in desperation as shimmery light bathed Stefan's face. I zipped off another spell as I wrestled with the creation aimed for Jonas.

"No. It's no good."

"Emmy." Jonas' voice was gruff, but the tone was pleading.

"Emmy is mine. That's the wonderful thing with fear and humans. They only have so much courage. And then they just wait to be led." Nathanial's voice was cold and grating.

I could barely see Emmy huddled against the wall. She held her whips to her chest. Her body racked in sobs.

"I overcame my fear, Emmy," I said with strain in my voice as I quelled the burns against Jameson's skin. Stefan tried to rush forward to physically kill Nathanial, but a singeing spell had him grabbing his eyes and staggering back.

"I am still terrified most of the time, but fuck it, you know? I'd rather be free in this life then caged in my old life. He only has the power over you that you give him. I've set you free—now you just have to keep your freedom."

I panted with fatigue. One of the mages in the corner passed out. Energy was scarce, even for Nathanial. The spells got more brutal. Wilder. More vicious.

Tim stood up and wobbled next to Stefan. Jameson and Jonas screamed and clutched at their heads, both having been hit with a spell I couldn't unravel in time. Charles tried to work another spell, pushed back with the effort. The spell scalded his shoulders.

We couldn't even get to him to push him over the ledge. We couldn't reach him, and I was no match.

I focused on a spell bubbling in front of Nathanial. I knew that mix of fire and earth. I knew Nathanial's love of acid.

He was about to kill everyone in this room, including his own people, and there was no way I could alter the spell to make it benign. I'd learned his magic, but he'd learned my tricks. He'd closed that vulnerability susceptible to my inverted magic.

"Get out! All of you!" I screamed.

"You see my spell, human?" That cold grin was aimed directly for me. Tim groaned and sank to the ground. Stefan's arms swirled with magic as he fought a spell. As he fought the pain. "What a lovely prize you would've been. Better-trained than I expected. But if you blow up this spell—why do Americans love blowing things up, I wonder—your explosion will simply kill the last mages connected to me as I erect my shield. Checkmate."

"Get out, Stefan, please!" I begged.

"Then what, love?" he asked with strain in his voice as he staggered. "With our last mage gone, who can stop him?"

"Toa!" I said with tears in my eyes. I worked at that spell as Nathanial finished it. As he held it in front of him for me to stare at in wonder. He was showing me how far above me he was. Ever the showman.

In desperation I tried to tweak it. Mess with it. But it was fortified and booby-trapped, just as Nathanial had said. Any heavy-handed magical attempt would blow it. We'd all still die, because I barely had anything left. I wouldn't be able to shield.

We'd all die.

I watched as that last fiber of the spell moved toward its home. The trigger.

A crack sounded behind us. Nathanial screamed and reached for his shoulder. The spell wobbled. A moment later a knife blossomed in the mage's throat. Another knife hit his eye and sank in deep.

The trigger still moved in as Nathanial slumped back against the wall.

"That spell is going to trigger!" I screamed. I ran forward, but Stefan was already there, Jonas and Jameson staggering after. Clenching their jaws against the pain, the three pushed through as a unit, forcing each other on. With a guttural yell, and braced by his two Watch Commanders, Stefan was pushed around that spell and at the slumping mage. He picked up the other man in a huge show of strength and tossed him out of the window.

I summoned every reserve I had and devised the equivalent of magical wind to blow that fog of spell out after him, pushing it out into the empty space over the battlefield as far as I could. The spell, 99.5% complete, and volatile because of it, exploded as its maker lost control of his magic.

As Nathanial fell, the explosion was directed skyward and out, raking down the sides of the building and punching at my weakening shield.

I braced and monitored my energy. I chopped off the links of everyone but Paulie and Birdie, the two strongest, and then I cut them off, too, as Nathanial's spell finally drifted away.

Panting, exhausted, I glanced around with wide eyes. Emmy stood at the back wall, straight-backed but visibly shaking. Her face was as pale as death. A whip dangled from a hand. Her other hand hovered next to her belt of knives. "I did it."

I lost sight of her as Stefan, once again, crushed me to his chest. We swayed together. I felt two hands come in to steady us—Paulie and Charles. "Jesus that guy was something."

"Someone needs to make sure he's dead." I buried my face into Stefan's chest.

"Oh yeah. He's dead. And his guys are—" Charles cut off as a huge explosion rocked the foundation.

"Oh no."

Everyone turned to a wide-eyed Emmy. Another explosion shook the building.

"He set traps. He was always setting traps. Without his magic to fuel the—" Another explosion. The building groaned ominously.

"Who cares why! Let's get the hell out of here!" Charles started sprinting for the door. Stefan pushed me in front of him.

We filed out as though the devil was on our heels. Another explosion and something structural popped. Wood squealed. Somewhere it sounded like crumbling stone.

"That guy was insane!" I yelled as I burst through the door into the main second-story hall. My legs shook under me. My energy was flagging badly.

Stefan picked me up and threw me over his shoulder in a fireman's hold. Only Emmy was faster than him. Jonas and the others were right behind, shifters included. Only Tim and Ann had had the strength and power to turn back into their animal form. The rest wobbled and staggered as fast as they could.

We took the stairs in a mad flight and fought a mass exodus as the building shifted. The floor dropped to our left: just sank down into the depths below. A gaping hole exposed moldy stone.

"Faster!" Emmy urged. "The whole place is going down. They didn't update the foundation when they re-did the living quarters."

A rumble tossed us to the side. Stefan grabbed a hold of me tighter and bounced off the wall. I felt another hand on my back that could've been Charles or Jameson.

"C'mon, man," Jonas growled from behind. I lifted my head to see Jonas ramming his shoulder under Paulie to keep him moving. "You're too big to carry."

Emmy slowed from in front of us and ran to Paulie's other side.

"Get out!" Jonas yelled at her.

Fierce determination written plainly on her face, she ignored Jonas and put Paulie's big arm around her shoulder. Together they rushed him up behind us as the whole place rumbled again. Dust filled the halls. More floor dropped out ahead. Ceiling started to rain down.

"Go right into that room. There's a hole that leads outside!" We could barely hear Emmy's voice through all the screaming.

Stefan did as she said, bursting away from the crowd and

through an open door. A beautiful, glowing hole greeted us where a wall used to be. Not wasting any time, Stefan plunged us through it and out through the crowds. There he turned left and kept running, pushing through. At the end he turned right again and slowed to an easy jog to the road.

"There. Nothing to it." He staggered to a stop once he reached the cement, gritted his teeth against pain he was still feeling, and put me down amid a sparse crowd of onlookers done with the fighting and just wanting to be out of the way. Most of them used to be the enemy. And we let them be. They weren't going anywhere.

Stefan set me down as I noticed someone I knew. My hackles rose and my jaw clenched.

That bitch.

Darla.

"Oh *hell* no!" She was dressed in a cute little sporty sweat suit and white shoes. She'd obviously run right out of the building by the safest route, and then stepped over here to wait patiently for a winner to be decided. Now that one was, she was probably thinking of sidling up to some Council members and slinking into their fold.

Well, screw that!

"Oh, Stefan." Darla sauntered closer with smoldering eyes directed at Stefan. "I see you're still toting your human luggage..."

My hands curled into fists. I stalked right up to her as the gazes around me started sticking to a face splattered with blood, dusted with dirt, and probably red with anger. I might not've looked hot, but I bet I looked pissed.

Darla smirked at me as I got right in her face. I cocked my fist and let it fly! I clocked her right in the nose. I heard a *crack* as her head whipped back. She staggered backward as her hands flew up to her face.

"Don't you dare think you are welcome anywhere on

Team Good-Guy!" I seethed. I concocted a mostly translucent box—I didn't have anything left—to keep her put and tied off the spell. Then, just to make sure no other magic users would come along and undo it, I put a bunch of flourishes and whatnot around the spell like Nathanial loved so much. He was a dick, but he knew his magic.

"Stay." I pointed at her like I might a dog.

Blood gushed down her lips and dripped off her chin. "You bwoke my node!"

"Why is it people always shout the obvious when they get hurt?" I turned to a grinning Stefan.

"Feel better?" he asked with a chuckle.

Jonas and Emmy jogged up with Paulie a moment later. Charles and a bunch of lagging shifters came seconds after that.

"Nice work, human." Jonas grinned at Darla as he put his arm around Emmy's shoulders. She leaned in heavily to his touch and closed her eyes.

"What'd you do? Punch her?" Charles asked, barely looking in Darla's direction.

"Yeah. She's a bitch." I slipped my hand into Stefan's and took Emmy's example by leaning heavily. I was tired, but I wasn't done yet. I needed a small rest before I let reality seep back in. Anger was a great distraction, but I had to face the outcome of the battle.

"Yes. She sure is. Can I just point out that you know how to punch because of me?" Charles preened.

"Can I just point out that the human did what you were too sissy to do?" Jonas countered. "How much blood did that wench get off you, again?"

"Says that guy that had to be saved by his girlfriend."

"She saved your ass, too, nitwit."

Charles rubbed his eyes. "Jonas, bro, I'm tired. Go find a

prison and lock yourself in. It was nice and quiet when you weren't around."

"The spell is fading," Jameson said with his hands on his hips. "That was a nasty one. Did you get it, Mage?"

I nodded with my eyes closed. "It was a nasty one. I know what he did, but I can't duplicate it yet. He was so far above me... I didn't know people could even *do* the stuff he put together. I have work to do."

"You'll get it." Jameson blew out a breath. "I'm glad he's gone, though."

"We all are." Jonas rubbed Emmy's back. I took that as a sign that the stalling had, once again, come to an end. I took a deep breath and started walking, my hand clutching Stefan's. I could hear the others fall in behind me. Even the shifters, who were gathering together as the battle wound to a close, followed our crew.

Bodies littered the ground leading up to the building. Those that were left alive were busy either securing the prisoners, running after prisoners, being prisoners, or just lying in a heap for medical aid. The building continued to groan and shift, parts falling down and wood or stone rolling from the structure. What was left was in no way salvageable. Someone would have to tear it all down and rebuild for the place to be habitable again. Which, I supposed, was a good thing. The Europeans would have to go elsewhere, though they probably had a few hideouts we didn't know about.

I vaguely watched three people chasing one large, male warrior through the cabbage field as I neared the place Cato and I had linked. And though he'd been removed, it wasn't hard to figure out where he'd gone. A collection of bowed heads gathered near the back of a van, all somber, a few crying.

I walked up slowly and was greeted by a grim-faced Toa and Dominicous.

"How is he?" I asked quietly, seeing the white head between the bodies as it lay in the van.

Dominicous reached out and ran his fingers down the side of my face. He let his hand settle on my shoulder. "He didn't make it." His eyes were soft and relieved as he looked at me, and though he wouldn't say it where we were standing, I knew he was intensely relieved I had pulled through. That if it was a choice between Cato and me, even though Cato was more valuable, Dominicous would've chosen for me to come out alive.

I stepped toward him and circled his waist with my arms. He hugged me tight. His cheek came down on my head. "Thank the gods you are okay," he said quietly, right next to my ear. "You scared me."

"I scared myself. Nathanial was... unreal. Far above anything I have seen."

"He's had a lot of experience," Toa said. I felt a light pat on my back. Toa's version of gushing. He was the creepy uncle in my life, and I loved him for it.

"But Cato had more." A pang hit deep inside me. I hadn't known Cato all that well, but what I did know, I really liked. He was a sweet, kind of senile guy with so much history and world experience. I wished I had a chance to get to know more of him. To learn more from him.

"He did, and he didn't," Toa said cryptically. "They were evenly matched at one time, but Cato's age caught up with him. He lived beyond his years. Nathanial was still in his prime. He was still experimenting and learning."

"Cato held on to pass on the most important of his knowledge—linking our kind to humans." Toa turned slightly to allow Mage June to join our small circle. Dominicous released me so Mage June could look directly into my eyes. The gaze held intense sadness, loss, uncertainty and a slight edge. "He imparted the knowledge of the black and white link. The magical yin and yang. Throughout the battle he muttered that you were a natural. That you took to it as if the danger wasn't an issue at all."

"Danger... wasn't an issue. Was it?" I scrunched my face up in confusion. "I mean, I got dizzy and whatever, but then... it was kind of like what I always had. Only, easier, kinda. It was more balanced. It *felt* natural."

"Yes, his point exactly. It took him ten years of study to link in that way without his spells morphing into something dangerous. Something that could kill him, his link partner, and everyone around them. When a person works with the other half of magic, inverting is always a huge risk. To invert is to create some horrible, unpredictable spells."

"Oh." I waved that thought away. "I've already learned that lesson. My teachers taught me like they taught their own kind. I set whole rooms on fire."

"Me, too," Paulie said from a few feet away.

Mage June's eyes flicked toward Stefan. I could tell it was a silent reprimand by the sudden stiffness of my mate and the defensiveness bleeding through the link. She focused back on me. "We will need to pick your next linking partner with care. It has to be someone both familiar with you, your type of magic, and—"

"It'll be Toa. Anyway, can I see Cato?" I interrupted. If she thought I was going to be sucked into the world of politics on the tail-end of a vicious battle where I lost one of my mentors, she was losing her mind.

Her lips turned into a thin line, but she moved aside slowly. Toa stepped closer and moved me closer to the van. In my ear, he whispered, "Cato was hoping for you and Stefan to one day take his and Mage June's role. You two will have a lot of interest from the Council. I would be wary, were I you."

"Not in the mood, Toa."

My breath caught as people stepped out of the way and I

saw Cato. He lay on a pad. His eyes were closed and hands crossed over his chest. He looked so peaceful, as though he were sleeping. But his chest was still. There was no rise and fall of breath.

Tears sprang to my eyes. "Does he have any family or anything?"

"No. His mate lost her life in childbirth along with the child. He never re-mated or adopted any other children." Toa stared down at Cato with glossy eyes. "He was my mentor. When I first started working with magic, he saw my potential and worked with me. He'll be greatly missed."

"Yet you didn't want to be his mage?"

Toa steered me away so others could pay their respects. "He already had Mage June. Plus, he knew I wanted to be in the thick of things. I wasn't meant for stuffy meetings and staying in one place for long. I was meant, instead, to find you. And pass on my teachings."

He led me away from the others a little. We turned toward the cabbage field, which was mostly demolished near the road, and stared out for a while in silence. A few more people had made a run for it, but it looked as though they'd been caught, hog-tied, and left to think over their life's choices, because they lay in heaps sporadically through the field.

"You were certain what you said to Mage June—you trust me to engage in the deep link?" Toa's voice sounded wispy and uncertain.

I crinkled my eyebrows as I glanced over at him. "Yeah. Who else? By now you know how much I eff-up. I figure you're the only one who won't throttle me inside the first minute."

"I have less patience than others."

"Well, whatever. You're family. And I think you have a better handle on how my magic works than others."

"Yes."

He fell silent again, staring out. The crinkle in my eyebrows got deeper. I didn't say anything this time, though. The guy was grieving—he was allowed to be weird. We were all strung out and flipped around—I doubted anyone would be right for a while.

"I am honored that you call me family," Toa said finally. "And once we are recuperated, we will attempt the link in a safe location. Thank you for bestowing such a deep level of trust for me. Excuse me."

I must've looked like I was trying to solve a difficult riddle as I watched Toa stiffly walk away, because when Stefan appeared at my side, he said, "He acting weirder than normal?"

"Yeah. Way weird. I get the feeling that he's half afraid of that magic merge... thing."

Stefan glanced toward Toa as Ann trudged up to my other side.

"I think it's hilarious that those guys took off running through an open field as if no one would chase them." Ann pointed at another guy who'd made a run for it. About a hundred yards away, he quickly changed direction. Someone popped out of the cabbage and gave chase.

"The yin and yang of magic is a terrifying thing for people that know absolutely nothing of human magic." Stefan watched the chase in progress. "They know the dangers of inverting, but not the result. We've been taught since we were little that inverting magic is a life-ending situation. Until you did it regularly, and then the rest of the humans, we didn't realize the explosions and angry flora that result aren't the disastrous situation we were led to believe."

"So why is Toa freaking out?" I asked as I leaned against his arm.

"He has the potential to mess up as badly as you always do." Ann ran her hands through her shock of blue hair.

"Yeah. He's probably afraid you'll say 'I told you so'," Charles added from behind us.

I sighed. "Let's get home. I'm exhausted and I miss my babies."

Stefan kissed me on the head and turned to lead the way when Ann said, "Can I ride with you guys? Tim got a shallow knife wound and you would think his arm was falling off. The man is such a baby with the small stuff."

"What are we going to do with Emmy?" Charles wanted to know.

Jonas still had his arm around his new love-interest and was following the group's movements at a small distance. I didn't think it was because of the alone time, though. I had a feeling Emmy wasn't comfortable being in the presence of Stefan and Charles. Maybe even Ann. I was too tired to force my sparkling wit on her just now, though. I'd have to wait until I got some sleep and some coffee.

"Let Jonas sort it out." With a last glance at the crumbling building, we headed to our cars and what would hopefully be a stress-free few months to follow.

CHAPTER TWELVE

"I've never been anywhere where things were so... lax." Emmy huddled next to Jonas as everyone got out of the cars at the Mansion. From what the Boss said, they only had about half of their force returning right now. The rest were left behind to collect any that didn't make it. With the amount of bodies strewn around, Jonas had every reason to believe it would be a black few months to follow as they mourned their lost.

At the moment, though, Jonas could barely keep his eyes opened. He hadn't slept soundly since he'd been taken. On top of that, he'd battled. He was on empty.

"Sasha is a rare breed. She needs things to stay light and easy or she gets bogged down with the pressure. If she spends too much time in her head, she makes mistakes. She's in charge, but it helps to often let her forget it."

"And Stefan—the Boss?"

"It doesn't help for *anyone* to forget that he's in charge. Except Sasha. He bends whichever way she pushes him, generally. Lax around Sasha, alert around the Boss."

Emmy shot her eyes to the ground as the Boss strode by with a nod to Jonas. Sasha trailed behind, pale and weary. She stopped briefly in front of Jonas and Emmy. To Emmy she said, "I'm full human. Totally, one-hundred percent human. I didn't even know Stefan's people *existed*. The humans wandering around here are the same. When we're not treated equal, we kick someone in the balls. Well, the others do. I earned my place. I zap them with magic. Anyway, my point is, you will only be *lesser* as long as you think that of yourself. No one else will see that about you. Hell, you have half their blood—you're one step above me. And Paulie has already led the way on that score. Plus, he got someone pregnant—but don't talk to him about it, because he's totally freaking out about it. He was determined never to have kids. He totally likes the girl, and he's only ever with her now—they have an understanding, which she is apparently fine with her since he can give her babies—but she's pressuring him to mate, and he —totally freaking out. Anyway, my point is, you will be like gold. People will be knocking on your door to try and get at your womb. It's freaking weird, but there ya go."

Sasha paused and rubbed her hands over her face.

"Did you just say people would try to get at her *womb?*" Charles asked, aghast. He hovered right behind Sasha.

Ann punched him in the side as she passed. "She's divulging some heavy shit, Charles. Let the lady work." Ann snickered and moved up the steps to the Mansion. "Sasha, you need to sleep. Seriously, you're losing it."

"You agree with me, yet you still punched me and argued?" Charles stalked after Ann.

"You're an idiot."

"What does that have to do with anything?" they barely heard as Charles and Ann went through the door.

Sasha stared at Emmy with bloodshot eyes. "What I mean is, you're welcome here. You'll fit in as soon as you stop cowering. Because if you cower, people will think they rock, and that is no good. It goes right to their heads, and then they'll get kicked in the nuts when they try to put that on another human. And when people veer away from you, it isn't you. It's Jonas. He scares people. They'll think you're a tough bitch just dealing with him. Also, you have the weekend off, but then you best get in school. You need to earn your keep, and Jonas thinks you're strong in power, so that's good. We can use you."

"You're babbling, human." Jonas shooed Sasha toward the door. "Go see your kids. I'll be by tomorrow to hold one."

"Oh no. Can't just take one. You'll take both or none. Do my job, or don't. No halvsies just because you're boinking a halvsie. Get it?"

Sasha's shoulders drooped and she shook her head. "Yikes. I'm tired. See ya."

Jonas smirked as he led Emmy up the steps to the front door behind Sasha. They went down the hall slowly so Emmy could take in the Mansion, and then turned up the stairs toward Jonas' quarters. "Do you mind staying with me? We can have a room made up for you tomorrow if you want your own place."

"With you is fine."

Jonas gave her shoulders a squeeze as they walked down the corridor. As Sasha had said, people saw him coming and immediately hustled to the sides to be out of his way. Most had probably been tossed through a door at one time or another and didn't want a repeat. It made Jonas' life easier.

"She seems nice. Weird, but nice," Emmy said quietly. "And the Boss seems to really dote on her."

"Yeah. They make a good team."

"Is what she said true—are those with human blood sought after because of their ability to reproduce?"

Jonas couldn't help stiffening slightly. He wanted this female more than he'd wanted anyone in his whole life. Being near her, hearing her voice, breathing her scent—she felt like a piece of him. He wanted to mate her, mark her if she'd let him, and see if they could bear children. But what he didn't want, and didn't know if he could handle, was someone else trying to get at her or her brood. He didn't think he could share. Not her.

"Toa is thinking that our stunted reproduction might have to do with staying to ourselves. We don't inbreed, obviously, but we don't have a lot of input from diverse regions. Humans are great at reproduction anyway, and they are fresh blood. Toa thinks that helps. I, personally, think humans are great at populating. That's their defense against a harsh environment."

"Nathanial kept me to himself all these years to try and get me with child. He thought the child would lean toward his race. Yours. Then he was afraid he might be the problem, and didn't want anyone else to touch me."

Jonas felt a pang in his chest for her treatment. He squeezed her before he opened his door and waited for her to go in ahead of him. Once the door was closed behind him, he said, "At least you only had one tyrant, rather than multiple."

Emmy nodded as she wandered into the room, the weight dragging down her shoulders relenting for the first time since she'd met his people. She sighed and then giggled. Hurrying to the other side of the moderately-sized room, she ran her fingers over his various sexual tools, a stand not unlike hers in the dungeon.

"And now I see." She leaned against the wall as she fingered the paddle. Heat crept into her gaze. "I know you're tired, but take off your sweats and get on your knees. I want to punish you. Then let's see if you can get me pregnant before we go to sleep."

Jonas went from dead-tired to wide-awake with a hard-on in the time it took him to strip his sweats. He knelt right where he stood, doing as she said. He gulped as she released a heavy leather paddle from the stand. His heart started to beat as she stripped out of her blood-spattered dress and stood before him completely in the nude. His stomach flipped as she sauntered toward him with all the command and grace as the first day he'd met her. This time, however, she wasn't ashamed of her sexual nature. This time, she was exploiting it.

"You're so beautiful," he said in a gush.

"I didn't say speak." She swung the paddle with force. The leather slapped against his stomach. Pain lanced out across his skin.

"Yes, ma'am."

"I said, I didn't say to *speak!*"

He heard her giggle right before the paddle slapped across his back. He clenched his jaw and squeezed his eyes shut, soaking into that pain. Feeling it morph into adrenaline. Feeling his dick lurch, begging to touch this beautiful, commanding female.

"Good." She slapped him across his butt, and then again on his shoulder. He could hear her breathing speeding up. Hear her excitement. She loved being in control. He loved when someone else took the reins. She felt free, and he was free within the confinement. She needed to hold the power to escape her past, and he needed someone to rein him in to quell the violence raging in him from his. They fit perfectly. They were made for each other.

"I love you," he said without meaning to. "I want to mark you."

The leather paddle hovered in the air as she stared down at him. Incredulity and uncertainty mingled on her face. "What did you say?"

"Nothing," he said quickly. He dropped his head. He didn't even know how she felt—if she felt anything. He could've just been her meal-ticket out of her situation.

Way to jump the gun you idiot!

He felt the sting of the paddle. "What did you say?"

To his silence he felt it again. And again. More violent now. He felt her power humming through him. His dick was so hard it was painful.

"Tell me!"

"I love you and I want to mark you," he blurted. "Please touch me, baby. *Please*."

The paddle dropped to his side in a collection of dull thunks. One of her palms slapped the top of his head and pushed his head back. Before he could blink, she bent to his neck in a rush. Her hot breath soaked into his skin before her teeth bit into him. The sweet draw from her mouth was pleasure unlike he'd ever experienced. His eyes fluttered closed and he moaned.

She straightened up and walked quickly to the bed. Her perfect body settled into the middle with her legs bent and slightly spread. Her fingertips trailed down between her breasts. "I love you, too. And I accept."

Something washed over Jonas. A primal need to take his female. To make this female his. Forever.

He rose on smooth joints and eyed her pale skin amid his crimson sheets. His cock pulsed. His stomach twisted with anticipation. His senses sharpened. A thrill coursed through his body.

Her breath quickened as he approached. Wariness flashed in her eyes before heat-soaked desire took its place.

Mine.

In a gush of speed, Jonas was on her. He pushed her body into the mattress, trapping her under him. Her thighs were pushed wider to accommodate his size. He captured her wrists and held them above her head. With a quick thrust, he entered her fully, stretching her to fit his size. Her heart rapped against his chest. The vein at her neck throbbed.

"You're mine." He almost didn't recognize his voice through the possessive gruffness. Through the raw, unyielding desire. "Forever."

He bit into her neck and took her blood in greedy gulps. He thrust into her repeatedly, hard and fast, feeling the friction of her body against his sensitive skin. He took his prize as the animalistic secretion in his skin permeated hers. He was laying his mark. If anyone touched her from this day on, he'd kill them without asking questions.

"Yes," Emmy sighed.

Jonas pumped into her harder. Into his female. Her heat, her wetness, overcame him. He drew once more on her neck, savoring that wild, battle-laden taste. His hard length seared into her soft depths. Faster and harder. His skin slapped off of hers. His bed squealed in protest.

"Yes, Jonas. Please, *yes!*"

"Take more of mine," he commanded. He bent so she could reach his neck.

Her draw was such succulent pleasure. It reached down through the core of him. An orgasm rocked his body. He emptied himself into her as she trembled in completion under him. The last of his mark settled firmly into her. His lips sought hers with a deep, lingering kiss.

After they were done, she shifted a tiny bit to get comfortable with his weight, and stroked his back. "It's kind of late to ask, but are you sure?"

Jonas huffed out a laugh. "I was thinking of asking you the same thing, but I was worried you'd say no."

"I'm not worried. Not at all. You don't scare me. I don't mind when you overcome my strength—it's hot. I don't care if you get bossy, or command me—I *know* you. I feel like I've known you all my life. I worried that once you got me home, though, you wouldn't want me."

"I should've waited. I should've let you have a taste of your freedom before I shackled you."

"You are my freedom. I hope I can give you a baby."

"It doesn't matter. If you do or don't, it doesn't matter. I have you. And I'm an uncle, of sorts. That is more than I'd ever thought I'd have. I'm the happiest in this moment than I have ever been. And if you tell Charles any of this, I will never speak to you again."

Emmy blurted out a laugh. "I'm excited to get to know your friends. They aren't what I'm used to."

"They aren't what anyone's used to. Trust me. And that's how I know that I fit in this life. With them. Where I am. I've finally found a real home."

EPILOGUE

I leaned back in the overstuffed sofa as my twin three-year-olds fought over some stupid toy drum. Why Charles insisted on giving them the loudest presents he could find, I did not know, other than he thought it was outrageously funny. Which it wasn't.

"Mommy!" Sabrina yelled. "He took my drum!"

"Share, you guys!" I shouldn't yell at them. I knew this. It was not only frowned upon, but also terrible parenting. But seriously: I'd been hounded by Toa all day about my and Stefan's duty to move up to *at least* Regional; I'd dealt with a huge fight of humans versus non-humans; and I'd found some dumb kid in the park playing with circles and trying to call demons. Thank God the kid was a nitwit and had no sense whatsoever or he might've succeeded. Instead, he lost two days of memory and all his silly witchcraft stuff. I was equally grateful he didn't notice Charles and Jonas because it meant I didn't have to take him into our fold and train him with magic.

Speaking of human magic-workers, we had a great many. We were looking for humans around the age of puberty, now.

Grab 'em when they were young and so we could start training when their magic manifested—we called it an after-school club. And it was really working. A new mansion one town over was being built. The rights to the larger territory were being squabbled over. And by squabbled, I mean fought over. Whenever Stefan and I showed up, though, the opposing clan took off. They didn't have a mage or solid leadership. We had a black who had fought in some hairy battles and a leader who the Council was trying to groom to one day take over Cato's role.

It wasn't rocket science as to who was going to win the skirmishes.

Stefan and I were happy at the moment, though. We had a "moderately" sized house in the upscale part of town with five bedrooms, a playroom, and a score of other rooms. Anything compared to the Mansion was called moderate, I found out. If it was just our immediate family staying there, we wouldn't need a quarter of the space. But, of course, we had a great many more people who made our home theirs on a regular basis, so I was glad in the end we got a large place.

"Mommy! She punched me!"

"Sabrina, don't hit your brother!"

A knock on the door prevented me from moving. The drum forgotten, my exuberant kids went sprinting for the door.

"Ask who it is!" I shouted after them.

I never used to yell and shout this much. I really didn't. What was it about kids that made a person want to yell all day?

"Who is it?" Sabrina asked in a sweet voice. That was the voice she used right before she stabbed you. Which was why Jonas stopped giving her anything sharp: she'd gotten Stefan's violent side.

"Who goes there!" Savion demanded. He wanted to wear

capes all day. Because I only thought of Trek every time I thought of a cape, I tried to dissuade him.

"The boogeyman," came Charles' muffled voice.

"Oh good, I wanted to see him." Stefan sauntered into the room wearing a fitted black shirt that showed off his flawless torso, and slacks that hugged his defined thighs and scrumptious butt.

"No kids in our bed tonight," I said in a throaty voice.

His gaze swiveled to me as Jonas and Emmy sauntered into the room after him. Jonas was holding his first-born, a two-month-old baby girl that looked just like her mommy. She'd be a beauty someday. The verdict was out on what kind of magic the baby would have until puberty, as was the case with my kids, but everyone wondered. There hadn't been so much mixed breeding in history as there had been in our clan —at least, Toa couldn't find any record of it in the scriptures. But with all the humans wandering around, and with the Mansion's sexual culture... yeah, we had a ton of kids. A TON of them. Stefan's people were insane with happiness. We had visitors from all over the country asking us how to snare humans. Also making the humans offers to move. It was ridiculous.

"Don't you guys have your own house?" I asked Jonas.

"Yeah. In the suburbs. But you don't need half this space." He settled next to me on the couch. Emmy took the chair to my right and leaned back.

"We do when you stay here more often than not." I rubbed my head. "I'm tired."

Emmy nodded and glanced at Stefan. She refrained from commenting. She'd mostly shed her shyness around Stefan, but she didn't often cut loose either. It was a slow process. In time she'd come around, but as it stood, she just let loose with the humans and Charles mostly.

Charles sprinted in growling like a bear. Sabrina squealed

and laughed in his arms. Savion came barreling after him. As soon as Charles was in the room, he stopped in the middle and jostled Sabrina. "I've got your sister. I've got your sister!"

Savion took a running leap and kicked Charles in the shin.

"Ow! You little rat." He put Sabrina gently on the ground as he sank to his knees and pulled Savion into a bear hug. Another knock sounded at the door before I heard it open.

"Must be Ann," Jonas muttered.

"Thank you, security." I grinned as Ann sauntered in with jet black hair. She'd given up the blue a while ago for pink. Then it went to purple before she settled on black. I suspected black was to cover up some mistake, but she assured me it was a conscious choice.

"Don't get my brother!" Sabrina ran in with a dagger.

"Grab her, grab her! Who left a dagger laying around?" I jumped up from the couch as Stefan swung his long arms toward her and scooped her up.

"No, baby. No swords until you get your magic." He gave her a kiss on the forehead and set her back down *sans* dagger.

He didn't yell nearly as much as I did. I had no idea how he kept his cool.

Undeterred, and with her brother still getting attacked by Charles, she ran at them with a determined expression and balled-up fists. She punched Charles in the arm and then wound up and kicked him right between the legs.

"Ow! No—not the balls!" Charles let go of Savion and crumpled to the ground. "White flag, white flag," he wheezed.

Savion, released, smiled at his sister before turning a gloating expression on Charles.

"Time out, you two. That is not nice!" I used my firm voice. They usually listened with the firm voice. And Jonas' stare.

I sighed and closed my eyes. "Who are we waiting for, again?"

"Ann's lover," Charles said in a sulky voice as he climbed, painfully, to his feet and took a chair.

"Tim's taking care of something, but he'll be here—" A knock interrupted Ann.

It had shocked me a little when Ann had first mentioned she was seeing Tim. He seemed a little too serious for her. After a couple months, it still shocked me. They didn't seem all that interested in each other. It seemed more convenience than anything. And for Ann, getting a rise out of Charles.

And it did get a rise out of Charles, even though he still maintained he didn't want anything permanent. He often glowered at Tim when no one was looking, and he badgered Ann about her boyfriend constantly.

Ann wouldn't admit it, but I had a feeling she was lonely, and she'd chosen someone she knew wouldn't work out long-term so she could wait for Charles. The way she looked at Charles, and the fact that those looks were often returned, spoke volumes. But, while Charles was definitely growing up, and he didn't get up to nearly as much Mansion sex as he used to, he just wasn't quite there yet. Men just took longer to come around sometimes. And this man most of all.

It was just a matter of time, in my opinion. They'd finally have a moment when neither could deny their mutual attraction, and then they'd be glued to each other. Just a matter of time.

Tim strolled in with Paulie and Selene. Their two-year-old boy was waddling right at their side.

"Mama, can we play?" Sabrina asked as Savion ran by. He stopped right in front of Todd, Paulie's son, and grinned.

"Wanna play?" Savion took off to the right. Sabrina ran by Todd's side, making sure he didn't fall.

"Hey Stefan, Sasha, Jonas, Emmy, Charles—" Tim nodded

to everyone. His soft brown eyes held Ann's gaze for a moment. "Hi beautiful."

Charles rolled his eyes.

"Are the witches coming?" Ann asked as she scooted over on the love seat for Tim.

"Which ones? The Mansion is full of them." Charles picked at his nail.

"Unlike you, who is full of *it*?" Ann smirked at Charles.

"Dinner should be ready in an hour. Drinks on the patio?" I stood and stretched my back. "Dominicous and Toa are already out there."

"Oh shit—you didn't say they were coming." Charles hopped up and started walking out.

"Language!" Ann scolded. "There are children present."

"What are you in such a hurry about?" I asked Charles as Stefan stepped behind me and started to knead my back. I leaned into his touch. I hadn't seen him for most of the night and I missed him.

"I heard Toa got that spell wrong because he inverted it and I wanted to make fun of him."

"Don't make fun of him!" I threaded my fingers into Stefan's and followed Charles out.

Dominicous stood by the large BBQ station with a glass of whisky. Toa sat in one of the cushioned patio chairs with a glass of wine. They looked up when we came through the sliding glass door.

"Hi everyone," Dominicous said lightly.

"Hey, Toa," Charles started. Jonas calmly handed the baby to Emmy. "I heard—Damn it, Jonas! Why'd you punch me, bro? That's fucked up!"

"Language!" all the parents yelled.

"*Messed* up." Charles rubbed his arm with a glower and settled into one of the many chairs.

A server distributed drinks from a side bar. After

everyone had gathered and had their drink of choice, I raised my glass of juice. "I have an announcement." Stefan rubbed my back as everyone turned to me expectantly. "I'm pregnant. Hopefully with just one, this time."

Everyone smiled and beamed, wishing me congratulations, except for one person. Toa gave me his customary stare as he said, "Sasha, while that is happy news, what about stepping up in your post? We could really use you."

"Hey Toa, I hear you blew up a whole room!" Charles boomed.

Jonas smirked as he took the baby back and smiled down on her. "That time it was warranted."

Laughing, I raised my glass. "To family."

"To family!" everyone chorused.

_*_*_*_*_*_*_*_*_*_*_*_*_

Thank you for taking the time to read my ebook.

Check out Charles (book 8):

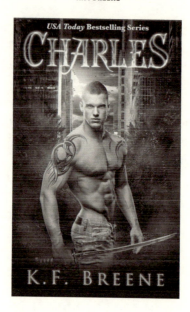

Never miss a new release or sale: http://eepurl.com/F3kmT

Website: Kfbreene.com
　Facebook: www.facebook.com/authorKF
　Fan and Social Group: https://goo.gl/KAgoNr
　Twitter: @KFBreene

Review it. Please support the book and help others by telling them what you liked by reviewing on Amazon or Goodreads or other stores. If you do write a review, please send me an email to let me know (KFBreene@gmail.com) so I can thank you personally! Or visit me at http://www.kfbreene.com.

Lend it! All my books are lending-enabled. Please share with your friends.

Recommend it. If you think someone else might like this book, please help pass the title along to friends, readers' groups, or discussions.

CHARLES (BOOK 8)

The story continues in:

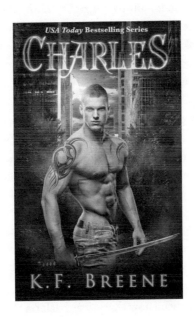

Excerpt:

Five hours and several glasses of wine later, Ann found herself stumbling outside for some air and a breather. Her head buzzed with alcohol and her lady parts buzzed with desire. She had guys doting on her constantly, excited with the rare prospect of getting to try a shifter in bed. She was the exotic party favor.

Strangely, in the mood she was in, she was totally okay with that. All she had to do was point at the person she wanted, and she would get him. Or them. In true Mansion fashion, they were okay with sharing.

She closed the sliding glass door behind her. She needed a break.

A giggle sounded off to her right, followed by a masculine hum. Ann veered to the left, feeling the cool breeze against her fevered skin. She lifted her hair off the nape of her neck and leaned against the wall of the house as her gaze traveled the shimmering swimming pool.

"Ann?"

Ann glanced to where a man and a woman stood in the faint light of dawn. The drop-dead gorgeous woman gave a whine of disapproval as Charles stepped forward. The light splashed across his handsome features, illuminating his smoky, grey eyes. Without saying anything to the woman he was with, he started across the patio to Ann, his huge breadth of shoulder drawing her gaze and setting her core burning.

"I haven't seen you all night," Ann said in a voice much huskier than she'd intended. "I thought you'd be all over it, trying to get a piece now that I was back on the market." Ann saw the woman pulling the strap of her dress onto her shoulder. She adjusted her breasts before heading back inside.

Ann's confidence withered. "Ah." She looked back over the pool. "You didn't want to wait that long, I gather."

Charles' eyebrows pinched together as he glanced behind him where the woman had been. "Oh no—she was just showing me her tits to try and get some."

"I'm amazed you could restrain yourself," Ann said, rolling her eyes.

Charles shrugged and leaned beside her. "She had a nice rack, but I've seen it before. Literally. A million times. I'm the last of Sasha's bodyguards to get tied down. They all want me."

"Should I step away—give your ego more room?"

"Nah. I'm bored with all the attention, now. At first it was cool. I mean, being a bodyguard was a shit job, right? It was embarrassing. But then she became a black mage, and the leader. Now I'm hot shit in this role. Even the humans want me—to get them knocked up, I mean. I can't find the thrill in it, anymore, though. And I don't want to get attached to some human. They always expect to mate the father. Not interested."

"Wow. Hard life."

Charles sighed. "Yeah. I mean...look at me! I'm walking around the place like a freaking disco ball. I got most of it off, too, and still I shimmer. Jonas punches me every time he sees me."

Ann couldn't help laughing, her dour humor lifting despite herself.

"Oh sure, mock me. But do you get showered in glitter? Doubt it." Charles ran his fingers through his hair. "Anyway, I was giving you space. Sasha said you needed some *you* time. Needed to choose your guy, or whatever. I'd hate to distract you with the glitter arms."

Ann laughed harder. "Lemme see."

Grinning, Charles sauntered in front of her to give her a

better view and put out one of his arms, which lit up like a Christmas tree as the light played across the multi-colored glitter. "Sexy, am I right?"

"It is all over?" Ann asked between large, belly laughter.

"Yeah." He stripped off his shirt, exposing his broad shoulders and defined chest. Perfect pecs led down into a deliciously ripped six-pack—actually, almost an eight-pack. Tattoos swirled around his arms and dotted his torso.

Suddenly, she knew exactly why the girls had put glitter on him. That perfect body gleamed and sparkled. If he were in the throes of sex, it would also glisten. Her mouth turned dry as her fingers itched to touch that smooth skin, cut and defined in all the right ways. Tim had been muscular, too, but not like this. Charles was so tall and broad, so powerful, but sleek as well. He moved like a dancer. A lethal, efficient dancer.

"Light up your tattoos," Ann said in a breathy voice as her gaze roamed his torso.

Deep orange swirled around his arms, playful and light. The magic tickled her animal side, her magic responding to his in ways that were supposed to be completely foreign, but for some reason, seemed as perfect as his body.

As his humor.

As his personality.

God she wanted this man. Had for years. She'd always said no to his advances because she knew she'd fall just that little bit more, and he didn't want to get attached. He'd just affirmed it a moment ago—not even a child would make him want to mate. He wanted his independence, and he wanted to bed whoever he chose, whenever he chose. Everyone in the Mansion knew that. It was only the humans who had a problem with it.

Ann sighed, feeling the fire as she looked over his delicious body. Then she came to a decision. Just this once, she wouldn't back away. Just this once, she'd give in to the thing he'd been trying to get from her since he first saw her.

She'd give in to him, just this once.

"Come closer, Charles..."

_*_*_*_*_

Buy it now: Charles

ABOUT THE AUTHOR

K.F. Breene is a USA TODAY BESTSELLING author of the Darkness Series and Warrior Chronicles. She lives in wine country where over every rolling hill, or behind every cow, an evil sorcerer might be plotting his next villainous deed while holding a bottle of wine and brick of cheese. Her husband thinks she's cracked for wandering around, muttering about magic and swords. Her kids are on board with her fantastical imagination, except when the description of the monsters becomes too real.

She'll wait until they're older to tell them that monsters are real, and so is the magic to fight them. She wants them to sleep through the night, after all...

Never miss the next monster! Sign up here!

Join the reader group to chat with her personally: https://goo.gl/KAgoNr

Contact info:
kfbreene.com/
kfbreene@gmail.com

OTHER TITLES BY K.F. BREENE

<u>Fire and Ice Trilogy</u>
Born in Fire
Made in Fire
Fused in Fire

<u>Finding Paradise</u>
Fate of Perfection
Fate of Devotion

<u>Warrior Chronicles</u>
Chosen, Book 1
Hunted, Book 2
Shadow Lands, Book 3
Invasion, Book 4
Siege, Book 5
Overtaken, Book 6

<u>Darkness Series</u>
Into the Darkness, Novella 1
Braving the Elements, Novella 2
On a Razor's Edge, Novella 3
Demons, Novella 4

The Council, Novella 5

Shadow Watcher, Novella 6

Jonas, Novella 7

Charles, Novella 8

Never want to miss the latest? Sign up here!

Check out her website: kfbreene.com

Made in the USA
Columbia, SC
26 July 2025